Cleaning Up Finn

"This romp of a noir through Southern California's South Bay will stay with you, challenging your ideas of poetic justice and leaving you wanting more from Sarah M. Chen."

—James W. Ziskin, author of the
award-nominated Ellie Stone Mysteries

"Readers will enjoy watching Finn Roose, a self-deluded ladies' man, bumble from one mistake to another, trying to hide his involvement with a missing teenage girl. A great read."

—Travis Richardson, author *Lost in Clover*

"Chen is a writer to watch."

—Matt Coyle, author of the Anthony
Award-winning Rick Cahill crime series

"Lives are shattered and bullets fly through the salty ocean air in this fast-paced debut from Sarah M. Chen."

—S.W. Lauden, *Bad Citizen Corporation*
and *Crossed Bones*

"A gritty and compelling journey, Chen navigates the intricate labyrinth of great modern storytelling with believable style."

—Darrell James, author of the
award-winning Del Shannon series

CLEANING UP FINN

Janet, so nice meeting you!

SARAH M. CHEN

CLEANING UP FINN

Second Edition, September 2017

All Due Respect
An imprint of Down & Out Books
3959 Van Dyke Rd, Ste. 265
Lutz, FL 33558
www.DownAndOutBooks.com

Edited by Chris Black and Chris Rhatigan
Cover design by JT Lindroos

ISBN: 1-946502-49-9
ISBN-13: 978-1-946502-49-0

For all the hard-working restaurant workers out there, especially the crazy folks I worked alongside for many years, slinging food and pouring drinks.

ONE

For the third time that day, Finn Roose regretted hiring Emily as his hostess. Sure she had big tits, but man, she had an irritating knack for interrupting him just when he was about to score a number.

Like now, for instance. The smoking hot redhead in the center booth, the one he'd been working the entire lunch rush—shit, for the past month actually—was just about to give him her digits when Emily swooped in and ruined everything.

"Mr. Roose?" Emily tried her best to wedge herself in between Finn and the redhead's table. "Some guy is on the phone for you. He's kinda hard to understand."

Finn's face tightened, trying desperately to ignore her childish voice. He remained focused on the redhead, her cleavage specifically, and stretched his smile until his face hurt.

"We can go out on the boat tonight, darling," Finn purred, angling his body away from Emily. He touched the woman's pale bare arm. Just enough to give her a taste of what would be in store for her later. God, she had soft skin. "If you would just give me your—"

"Do you want to take it?" Emily continued, undaunted.

The redhead was now looking at Emily, uncertainty clouding her face, and Finn knew he'd lost her. He dropped his business card on the table, the special one with his cell phone number on the back, and said, "Call me." The redhead barely acknowledged him with a slight nod. Christ.

"Take a message, hon," Finn ordered Emily. The restaurant was emptying, signaling the lunch rush was over, and he would need to start cashing out the servers.

"But he seems really anxious to talk to you," she said.

"Then he'll leave a message." Finn headed to the host stand at the front of the restaurant with Emily trailing behind him. He smiled at the guests who were leaving; this was supposed to be Emily's job for god's sake. "Good-bye, thanks for coming." Finn nodded to the business suits pushing through the glass doors that led outside to the parking lot and the marina beyond.

He noticed the redhead and her lunch buddy

were heading to the back of the restaurant, probably for the restrooms. Maybe he could have another crack at her before she left.

But after taking off a pizza that wasn't to table twenty-one's liking and comping a sundae for a birthday girl on table fifty-nine, there was no sign of the redhead. He'd missed her. Hopefully she'd be back for her weekly lunch next Tuesday with her co-worker. Or preferably alone. Finn didn't even know her name yet.

He noticed Tomas, his bartender from the Ukraine or Hungary or whatever fucked-up shit country he was from, unceremoniously drop the bill off at a posh-looking couple without so much as a smile or "thank you." Finn gritted his teeth. He'd just had a talk with the kid the other day about customer complaints of his surliness and bad attitude. "All you have to do is smile," Finn had instructed for the hundredth time. "Is that so hard? To fucking smile?" He wasn't even sure if Tomas knew how. He was a hard worker, but shit, even Finn was nervous around him with that blank stare, monotone voice, and imposing six-foot-four frame. He'd even heard rumors Tomas had been in prison, back wherever the fuck he was from.

Frustrated with everything, he settled himself into his cramped office and Jason, his takeout server, appeared in the doorway, holding his receipts and cash in one outstretched hand.

"Ready for me?" Jason asked.

"Sure," Finn responded with a tired 'come on in' wave.

After Jason, two more servers appeared, hovering in his doorway. The next hour zoomed by as Finn cashed out server after server. Marisa was the closing lunch server and when she showed up with her receipts, he knew it was about four o'clock. He was ready to go home. Maybe call his buddy Porter to see if he was up for watching the Laker game at Sports Cove.

Marisa was chattering away as usual, and Finn tried his best to ignore her while he counted her money.

"And can you believe that poor girl is missing?" Marisa asked, shaking her head.

Finn froze mid-count and looked up at her. "What girl?"

Marisa's eyes widened. "The missing girl? It's been on the news all day."

Finn felt like his heart was beating inside his head.

"Uh, okay this is good. I gotta make a call. You can go." Finn practically shoved Marisa out the door.

"But you didn't even finish counting my money. I have to—"

"Just go, it'll be fine, sweetheart," Finn insisted. He slammed the door after her and swiveled to the small television in his office. He flipped quickly through the channels until he found a local news station.

A smiling anchor appeared, thanking Laura for her weather report. His jovial demeanor shifted to a serious look. Finn turned up the volume, leaning in closely.

"—that authorities are now treating as a missing persons case. If you've seen this young woman, please contact Redondo Beach Police. We have Susie Chin right now in Phoenix. Susie?"

Finn stared with horror at the picture of the familiar young girl, and then it cut to a perky Asian woman with a microphone. She was standing next to a middle-aged mousy woman and a hulking man with beady eyes who Finn assumed were the parents. The man's meaty hands gripped his wife's shoulders.

"Thanks, Bob. I'm here at the home of the young woman's parents in Phoenix, Arizona. Mrs. Havemeyer, when did you discover your daughter was missing?"

Susie thrust the microphone into the distraught

woman's face. Mrs. Havemeyer sucked in her breath and peered into the camera with her husband glaring right behind her.

"I—I waited for Rhonda to call me. But then three days went by and I didn't hear from her so—so I got worried." Mrs. Havemeyer sniffled. "I called her cell phone but she wasn't answering. I called her hotel, but they said she never checked out and—and all her stuff was still there. And now—now it's been five days and—"

"I want to know what the hell happened to her," the husband interrupted. "If I find out something happened or someone..." He clenched his teeth.

Susie waited, then when she realized the man wasn't going to finish, turned back to the camera. "Rhonda Havemeyer is supposed to be headed to Arizona State University next week. We pray she'll be found and reunited with her family. Bob, back to you."

Finn sank back in his chair as Bob launched into the next story about the Los Angeles County Fair. His whole body trembled as he turned the television off. He needed some air.

Finn hurried outside, telling Emily he'd be right back, and headed toward the U-shaped Redondo Beach pier walkway that bordered his restaurant, the Waterfront Grill, and the adjoining Waterfront

Hotel. He walked along the pier until he reached the busy arcade on the other side, the bark of nearby sea lions echoing in his head. He fumbled with his suit jacket, yanking it off. Shit. He was having trouble breathing.

TWO

Five days ago, Finn had met a young lady named Rhonda Havemeyer who told him, "Everyone calls me Ronnie."

He had spotted her the second she walked into his restaurant wearing a flowery sundress, cleavage bursting out of the low-cut front. She was a little heavier than he preferred, but she wore it well. She chose a corner stool at the bar. Tomas greeted her with his usual sullen toss of the cocktail napkin, making Finn cringe. They chatted briefly and she showed him her ID. Tomas returned with a glass of white wine. Finn was relieved to see she was at least twenty-one. She looked really young.

He kept his eye on her throughout the busy lunch. He tried to make eye contact, but she was engrossed in her paperback while picking at her seafood salad. She took her time eating and drink-ing like she had nowhere special to be. He noticed she had only drank half her glass of wine in an hour.

Finn was dying to talk to her but this was an especially busy lunch. It was Labor Day weekend so more tourists than usual were filling the restaurant. The hotel was fully booked too. He noticed several tables in Marisa's station were vacated but dirty dishes and wadded up napkins remained on the tabletops. Finn scanned the restaurant for Oscar, the busser responsible for her station, but as usual he was nowhere to be found. The guy was a lazy piece of shit.

"Hey, man, maybe you can hook me up with a room."

Speak of the devil. Finn turned to see Oscar standing right beside him with an empty tray dangling at his side. A stupid grin plastered on his face.

"Shut the fuck up, Oscar, and bus these tables." He resisted the urge to smack the busser across the face. "We have to get these people seated."

Oscar silently filled his tray with dirty glasses and carried them to the dishwashing area in the back. Finn followed him with his own stack of dirty dishes. When he transferred them to the stainless steel dishwashing area, Oscar stood there watching him, leaning against the counter.

"What are you standing there for, you idiot?"

Finn was livid. "Marisa needs your help."

"Two chicks, man." A lascivious smile spread across Oscar's face as he shook his head. "You dog, you." He narrowed his eyes. "You gonna share some of that or what?"

Finn knew exactly what Oscar was referring to. Late last night, Finn stumbled into the Waterfront Hotel totally trashed with two hot chicks, Ami with an "i" and Mandy—or was it Amy and Mandi with an "i"? Skipper, the night clerk, had been discretely hooking him up with free rooms for years, a definite corporate no-no. It had never been an issue until now, an issue Finn would handle right this second.

He slammed the tray into its holding bin hanging on the wall. Jason, his takeout server, flinched when he zoomed by with a tray of dirty dishes. Finn jabbed a finger in the air at Oscar and stepped right up into his face. He could smell pot on his breath.

"I want you gone right now." Finn felt a vein pulsing in his forehead. "Nobody threatens me. Least of all a fucking wetback. You're a worthless piece of shit and I want you out of my sight."

Oscar's grin faltered slightly and doubt clouded his beady black eyes. "I'll tell corporate."

"Go ahead. I'll phone them and tell them you're

coming." Finn knew the kid wouldn't. And if he did, corporate wouldn't give a shit what a lowlife stoner had to say about him. He was their top GM, had the best sales of any restaurant in their company. He was untouchable. "Now get the fuck out of my restaurant. You're fired."

Oscar wavered, his eyes darting around. The dishwashing area bustled with activity, the occasional server swooshing in and out through the swinging doors to dump dirty dishes off. Glasses clanged and water sprayed out of the nozzle, but nobody spoke. Finn felt every eye on him.

"Go." Finn pointed to the side door down the hall. "Come back tomorrow for your tips. Otherwise, I don't want to see your lazy ass around here ever again."

Oscar took one last look around, glared at Finn, and slunk down the hall toward the side door.

Finn turned to see his dishwashers staring at him. "What are you all looking at? Get back to work." He pushed through the swinging doors back into the roar of the busy restaurant. Un-fucking-believable.

He prayed the hot chick at the counter was still there and blew a sigh of relief when he spotted her. She was just about to pay her bill. He bolted over to her and snatched it out of her hands.

"Let me get that for you, miss," Finn offered, realizing he'd probably scared the shit out of her. His adrenaline from the encounter with Oscar had made him a little manic. He needed to take a breath and relax.

She appeared startled, her hands in the air as if she were still clutching the bill. Then she hiccupped loudly. She cupped her hand over her mouth, her dark brown eyes wide. "Oh, I'm sorry. I'm not used to so much wine."

Finn silently shouted hallelujah and slid into the barstool next to her, arm on the back of her chair. He couldn't believe his luck and exhaled slowly, willing himself to calm down. "So what's your name, darling?" he asked.

She giggled. "Rhonda Havemeyer. But everyone calls me Ronnie." She rolled her eyes. "Well, except for my dumb parents."

A warning bell went off in Finn's head. Nobody said "dumb parents" unless they were too young to vote. But he plowed on. "Hello, Ronnie, I'm Phineas Roose, general manager here at the Waterfront Grill and Hotel. But everyone calls me Finn." He smiled. "You live around here, Ronnie?"

"No. I'm just visiting. For a couple more days."

"You staying here at the hotel?"

"Oh no." Ronnie gave a little laugh, shaking her

head, but she didn't offer more.

"So where you visiting from?"

"Phoenix." She paused. "Arizona."

In case I don't know where Phoenix is, Finn thought. God, she was adorable. He slid his hand from the chair to rest lightly on her shoulder. Ronnie glanced at it but made no effort to move, an encouraging sign. "What brings you out to our quiet little Redondo Beach?"

"I'm just taking a vacation until I start ASU."

Finn flashed his most charming smile. Oh boy, a college student. How he did love the college students. They were at that ideal age, the perfect combination of naïveté and bold self-assurance. Eager to try anything.

"Do you like sunset sails? It's a great way to see the harbor, and I have my own boat." It was his buddy Porter's boat, which was practically the same thing.

"Oh, I don't know. I've got a lot to—"

Finn stood up slowly, letting his hand trace the length of her arm. "I'll be a perfect gentleman, I promise."

"Well, maybe tomorrow..."

Finn handed her a card with his cell phone number on the back. "I'll pick you up tomorrow night at six. Just tell me where."

THREE

The next night, giddy with anticipation of seeing Ronnie again, Finn pulled to a stop on Hermosa Avenue near the Hermosa Beach Pier in Porter's convertible red Ferrari California, top down of course. The pier was crowded with the typical beachgoers, couples, and twenty-somethings looking to party. Ronnie told him she'd meet him on the corner of Hermosa Avenue and Pier but didn't specify an actual building, so he waited in front of the Bank of America.

Finn scanned the pier but didn't see her. She was probably in Sharkeez where everyone under thirty hung out to get shit-faced and hook up. Then again, she didn't seem the partying type.

He glanced at the car's clock. Six-twenty. He wasn't *that* late. Maybe she thought he wasn't coming and left. He searched for his cell phone to see if she called him but after rummaging through the glove compartment and his jacket pockets, he realized he'd left it at home. Crap.

He did find Porter's black yacht cap on the floor of the passenger seat and plopped it on his head. Finn preened in his rearview mirror, adjusting the braided bill. Porter loved this cap, but shit, it looked so much better on him.

He spotted Ronnie in the rearview. That long blonde hair and sturdy build. She was about a block away talking to a young guy. Actually, it looked more like he wanted to talk and she wanted nothing to do with him. Finn was about to get out of the car, but luckily she saw him and hustled over, leaving the kid to ogle her ass.

She smiled, waving to Finn. Christ, she looked good. She wore a silky black pantsuit with a belt made out of giant silver rings that fit snug on her full hips.

"Nice ride," she commented as she slid into the passenger seat.

"Nice outfit."

She giggled.

"Anything I need to take care of?" he asked, pointing back at Frat Boy.

"Huh?" Confusion washed over her face, then she waved her hand. "Oh, no. He was harmless. An idiot, but harmless."

Finn shrugged, continued down Hermosa Avenue toward King Harbor in Redondo Beach. Ronnie's flowery perfume wafted through the car, an enticing mix with the balmy night and gorgeous leather interior.

A couple hours earlier, Porter had made Finn promise to furnish his own liquor for his seduction that night.

"I'm not kidding around, Finn," Porter had said when Finn called about using his boat and convertible. "I don't want you and your whore du jour touching a drop of my liquor, okay?"

Finn had assured Porter that this girl would be a two-drink sink, two drinks and down she goes.

Porter groaned but a chuckle escaped him. "And here I assumed you picked them solely for their looks."

Finn's best friend, *only* friend actually, never failed to remind him what an asshole he could be. But Finn and Porter went way back, all the way back to Elmwood Street where they grew up five houses down from one another. They bonded over a mutual loneliness, both of them being only children with absent fathers. They were inseparable from that point on, up until Porter left for Yale on a full scholarship.

Now years later, they were still best friends living within miles of each other in the South Bay. But that's where the similarities ended. Porter was married with a five-year-old son and an eighty-hour-a-week job as an entertainment lawyer. He didn't have the time to enjoy his forty-four-foot sailboat and cherry red Ferrari.

Finn worked hard too but made damn sure *somebody* had the time to enjoy the forty-four-foot sailboat and cherry red Ferrari. He felt the occasional pang of guilt for what some would call "taking advantage of a situation," but Finn reminded himself that Porter was just paying him back the only way he knew how.

When Finn and Ronnie arrived at King Harbor, he escorted her to the slip where the Moonshine, Porter's glorious boat, was docked. When she spotted the sumptuous spread of merlot, cheese, and crackers he had thoughtfully arranged earlier, her eyes lit up. She clapped her hands in glee.

"It's perfect," she gushed.

Finn motored the Moonshine out onto the water, invigorated by the ocean air and the anticipation of some action later. By the time he had the sails up and they were skimming across the Pacific Ocean the sun was already setting, a brilliant crimson and golden backdrop.

"What's that out there?" Ronnie pointed.

"That's Catalina Island, darling."

"I've been dying to go there. I heard it's so beautiful," she said with a sigh. Finn detected a wistful, almost sad tone in her voice. She better cheer up soon, he thought, or this was going to be a short boat ride.

"Omigosh, Finn, look!" Ronnie ducked down and then popped up from behind the bar with two glasses and a bottle of Dom Pérignon. Finn was horrified.

"No!" he cried in alarm.

She stared at Finn. "Why not?"

"Well because—uh, because we have wine," he offered lamely.

She giggled. "We'll drink that too, silly." She popped the cork and said, "Woo hoo!" She handed him a glass of the fizzy liquid. "Cheers."

"Cheers." Finn clinked her glass, and they drank.

And then they drank some more. The Dom disappeared within the first twenty minutes. When Ronnie opened Porter's hundred-dollar bottle of cabernet while Finn was busying himself with the boat, he had another moment of panic. Then he thought, what the hell? It's not like Porter couldn't afford to buy more.

The more Ronnie drank, the more she talked. The more she talked, the more Finn drank. He could barely keep up with this girl and he considered himself a professional. He even gave up on maneuvering the boat and let it just drift in the water. It required too much concentration, his mind clouding in a haze of alcohol. He plopped down next to her.

"Why aren't you married?" she asked in between gulps of wine.

Finn grimaced. The thought of one woman the rest of his life made his chest constrict and his vision blur. "I just haven't found the right woman yet, darling." He smiled at Ronnie. "They're not all as beautiful and fun as you."

She giggled and playfully shoved his shoulder. "Stop. You're so sweet." She sipped her wine, those dark brown—or were they black?—eyes watching him from the rim of her glass. "I just can't believe you haven't found the one yet. How old are you? Almost forty?"

He almost spit out the cabernet. Ouch.

"Isn't it time to settle down and have kids? Don't you want kids?"

"For starters, I'm twenty-nine." He was thirty-two but whatever. "So I have plenty of time to settle down and have kids."

A smile crawled across her face. "You don't even like kids, do you?"

"I like kids." Finn shrugged. He had worked in enough restaurants over the years to permanently turn him off snot-nosed brats who spilled crap all over his nice mahogany booths. Still, the fact she seemed to know exactly what he was thinking irked him. "Everyone likes kids."

Ronnie didn't say anything. She just studied him with that smirk on her face.

Irritated, Finn turned it around on her. "Well, *you* want kids, right? All women want kids."

"No...not every woman," she said, an edge to her voice. Her face darkened. "Maybe some women don't know what they want to do yet." Ronnie's voice became louder. "Maybe some women don't want to go to college to make something of themselves."

Finn gulped his wine, pretending not to notice her increasing agitation. Clearly, he'd hit a sore spot. ASU was obviously her parent's idea.

"Well, what *do* you want to do, darling?" He needed to calm her down and get her back into the mood.

"I want to travel. It'd be so cool to work on a cruise ship or be a flight attendant, you know? End up somewhere new every day." She gazed out at the tranquil water. "Or live on an island. Like that one out there." It was too dark to see it but Finn knew she was pointing at Catalina. "Drink rum and eat coconuts every day."

Finn doubted they had a lot of coconuts on Catalina Island but didn't want to ruin her fantasy.

"I want to experience life. Not bury my nose in a book or have kids." She shook her head. "My family doesn't get it. They don't get *me*." She grew quiet, staring into her wine glass.

Finn cleared his throat. "I know what you mean. My dad still doesn't get why I like working in the restaurant industry. It's like a stupid hobby or something to him." He was merely trying to make Ronnie feel better, but surprisingly, the resentment came tumbling out. He figured he'd gotten over it by now. He hadn't seen or heard from his dad in what—ten, eleven years?

His entire life, Finn had felt like a fuck-up and a disappointment. His father wanted him to attend Pepperdine. He pulled every string, bought a building, just to get his only child into a university he approved of, and Finn had to go and "fuck it up like he did everything else." His dad's exact words.

That Finn ran one of the busiest restaurants in the South Bay and pulled the top sales of all the restaurants the corporation owned didn't seem worth two shits to his dad. In his dad's eyes, he was a complete failure and always would be. A loser with nothing but a semester of economics and Italian cinema under his belt. Both classes he failed.

"My dad wanted me to be a lawyer like my best friend. Didn't matter that *I* had no interest in it," Finn continued.

Ronnie turned to him, eyes wide. She nodded enthusiastically. "Right?" She smacked the wood handrail with her palm. "My dad thinks I'm only good for getting pregnant and having kids." She shook her head, falling silent.

"To doing what we want, darling," Finn said, holding up his wine glass toward her.

"To doing what we want," she repeated, relaxing. They clinked glasses and Finn couldn't help thinking what he really wanted to do at that moment. He gulped his wine, set the glass down, and then reached around Ronnie's sturdy waist, pulling her closer. Surprisingly, she didn't resist and scooted across the seat toward him.

"I was wondering when you'd make a move on me," she said, her voice husky. Her eyes were half-closed, giving her face a dreamy cherub look. She turned to face him and shoved her tits into his chest.

Finn could feel the silly grin spreading across his face but didn't care. "C'mere, darling," he whispered. His hands roamed her body as he bent down to kiss her. Her mouth opened and her warm tongue slithered all over his teeth and his mouth and everywhere else. She wasn't the best kisser, a slobberer, but hey, he wasn't going to be picky. Shit, he was probably a sloppy kisser himself right now considering how much he'd drank.

After making out for about five minutes and groping each other, Ronnie surprised Finn by saying, "Let's go back to the dock…get a room at that cool hotel." She stood up.

Holy shit, that was exactly what he was thinking. He couldn't believe his luck and leaped to his feet, ready to haul ass back to shore, when he remembered there were no rooms at the Waterfront. It was Labor Day weekend and no way could Skipper pull it off for Finn. But hey, wouldn't a college kid enjoy a little sumpin'-sumpin' on a boat?

"We have a bed right here, baby," Finn purred, referring to the cramped bedroom quarters down below. Not ideal but it had its charm.

She glanced behind her down to the living quarters. "Umm…how about your place then? It would be more—uh, comfortable." Her hand gave his butt a tight squeeze.

"But it's so romantic on a boat." The last place he wanted to take Ronnie was his shithole of an apartment. He hadn't cleaned in days and normally he didn't even notice the mess, but he knew it was no place to seduce a woman.

Her hand made its way to his crotch, rubbing his hard cock. "Come on, baby, let's just get out of here."

Finn groaned. God, he wanted her so bad, he was ready to agree to anything. Almost. He tried to guide her toward the stairs but teetered and had to grip the handrail. Shit, he was plastered. Which gave him an idea. "I can't, darling, I'm totally hammered."

She pouted.

"C'mon, let's just do it here," he whispered in her ear. He stuck his hand under her shirt and squeezed one of her enormous tits. He couldn't wait to suck on them. "You're so hot, baby."

Ronnie giggled and allowed him to move her backwards until she was poised on the edge of the stairs. She swiveled her head around. "Wait, wait… I'm gonna fall."

Finn took her glass of wine and guided her down the stairs. It was awkward and narrow. She gripped the handrails, edging her way down slowly. Finn followed, surprised how much the boat was swaying. He even had to stop for a second and focus on the wooden steps. They seemed to be moving.

Ronnie reached the bottom and turned around. Finn handed her the glass of red wine so he could use both hands to walk down the stairs. Christ, he was all off balance. He practically shoved her toward the small bed that was built into the wall.

She started removing her pantsuit. Her cheetah-print bra disappeared too and those lovely breasts beckoned him like a lighthouse on a dark night. Finn fumbled with his pants and the boat lurched to the side. He stumbled and fell against the side of the bed, his head whacking against the wall.

Ronnie laughed and threw her pantsuit behind her, exposing matching cheetah-print bikini underwear. She climbed onto the bed and turned to him. "Come here, sexy." It came out as "C'mere, shex-shee."

"I'm trying, for Chrissakes," Finn grumbled. God, he was having a hell of a time. Was he really that fucked up? And did it always smell so musty down here? His stomach did a little churn and he feared he'd puke. He flopped down onto the bed.

Ronnie crawled over to him and Finn pulled her on top of him. "Oof," he said. Man, she was heavy. Her skin was soft and silky though, and he ran his hands up and down her fleshy backside. He kissed her hungrily. She moaned and thrust her hips into his. They ground their hips like that for a while and then she moved away. Finn felt her tugging his zipper. She pulled his pants down, boxers included. The girl was certainly eager. He closed his eyes, willing himself not to throw up, but everything was spinning and—

"What's wrong? Don't I turn you on?"

"Huh?" Finn opened his eyes to see his once-hard cock looking sad and deflated. No, no, no. "Come here, baby. It's fine. I just need to feel you." He tried to focus on her but there were two of her. Four giant tits flashed in front of him and he reached a hand out, only to collapse back as the boat rocked to the other side.

Ronnie—lordy, she was enthusiastic—climbed back on top of him and took his limp cock in her mouth. She really made a valiant effort but between the rocking boat and the spinning room, his dick just wasn't cooperating. Fuck.

She finally gave up and sighed noisily. "Is it me?"

"No, no, no." Finn struggled to right himself. "I just need some air. I—I just need to get the hell off this boat." He tried to focus on her blurry tits. He felt his dick stir. "Wait, I think he's awake."

Ronnie pounced back on top of him, rubbing his cock. She licked her lips and said, "Mmmmmm, like that, baby? Pretend I'm a porn star." She straddled him, grinding her hips into his and running her hands through her hair like she'd probably seen on Skinemax. "Just call me Cherry Nibbles."

"What?" He stifled a laugh. He was actually getting into her little act until she blurted that out. "Did you say nibbles or nipples?"

She stopped gyrating long enough to say, "Nibbles. You know how your porn name is the street you live on and your pet's name? Well, I live on Cherry Avenue and have a bunny named Nibbles."

She looked so serious explaining this that Finn didn't have the heart to tell her that it was the other way around. But hey, whatever got her off.

"Love it. Totally hot," he said. "C'mere, Cherry Nibbles." He grabbed her and pulled her down on top of him. He could feel her tongue licking him everywhere and slowly making its way down to his cock.

"Oh yeah," he moaned, closing his eyes. "Just like that." He scooted backwards to give her room on the bed and whacked the back of his head against the wall. "Fuck!" Now his head throbbed.

Ronnie tried to wake his cock up but it was no use. He heard her fumbling around for her clothes.

"I'm sorry, baby, I swear this never happens. Let's keep trying and I'm sure—"

"It's okay," she said, sounding disappointed. She'd already pulled her pantsuit on and stumbled up the narrow stairs to the deck.

"Cherry, come on!" Finn reached his hands up to her disappearing ass. "Nibbles?"

Nothing. She was over it already. Humiliated, Finn threw his clothes back on and crept up the stairs. As soon as he reached the deck, he breathed in deeply. The salt and briny air invigorated him and he felt a hundred percent better.

Almost. He was still plastered. Ronnie was standing at the stern, facing the harbor lights. Their glow fuzzed and faded, giving her a halo effect. She actually looked like she was floating. He shook his head, trying to regain focus. It was time to head back in and Finn wasn't sure if he would be able to dock the boat.

After what seemed like hours, Finn managed to maneuver the boat into the slip. Thank god nobody was around to see him bumping and whacking into the dock. Ronnie laughed hysterically at his pathetic attempts and he wanted to smack her.

Normally, he'd hose the boat down and clean everything up for Porter, but he was in no condition to do anything except pass out in bed. Finn wasn't sure how but they managed to get off the boat without breaking an ankle. They stumbled their way down the nearly deserted dock, holding one another up. When they reached the end of the gangway, she stopped. "My purse!" She started to head back, but Finn grabbed her arm.

"I'll get it," he mumbled.

"I'll be over here," she said. She continued toward the grassy area lining the walkway, weaving back and forth.

After several attempts, Finn managed to climb on to the boat without throwing up or falling overboard and found her big black handbag along with Porter's yacht cap, which he plopped onto his head. He hoisted her bag over his shoulder and carefully disembarked from the Moonshine. He dreaded the ride back with her.

When he decided that it was best to just end the night there and call her a cab, he realized he had almost reached the end of the gangway but there was no sign of Ronnie. She had vanished.

FOUR

"Ronnie? Finn squinted, stumbling forward down the gangway. It shifted slightly in the water, and Finn felt the cheese and crackers from earlier churn in his stomach.

He scanned the marina as best as he could with it moving in and out of focus until he thought he saw something about thirty feet away. Ronnie? Finn stumbled over to find her lying face first in the grass.

"Ronnie?" Finn shook her shoulder, but she didn't respond. Goddammit, seriously? Was she dead? Panicked, Finn touched her warm neck and was relieved when he felt her pulse.

"Ronnie, wake up," Finn pleaded. He slapped her cheeks gently a few times. Nothing. Shit, shit, shit. He gave her a good *whack* on the face just in case, but she remained lifeless. Finn fumbled around for his cell phone but remembered he'd left it at home like an idiot. Who would he even call anyway? Porter? Wake him up in the middle of the night and ask him what—to come out and help him put this girl in his car? His wife, Lana, would love that. She already thought Finn was a loser.

There was no choice. He had to carry her. Bring her to his place himself. He looked her over, guessing her to be about one-fifty, maybe even one-sixty. Okay, no problem. He had a slim build but worked out enough to consider himself fairly fit. His back wasn't in the best shape, but he would be careful to bend his knees.

He put his arms underneath her and groaned, struggling to lift her. Holy crap, she was heavy. He managed to heave her slightly off the damp grass. He was in a sort of crab-like crouch when he felt himself pitching forward. Oh shit, oh shit, oh shit. He ended up dropping her and falling on top of her.

Okay, no way he was picking her up. His back was already starting to ache. He felt more than his thirty-two years. He noticed Porter's yacht cap had fallen off and stuck it back on his head.

She needs to go back to her hotel, he thought. Problem was he had no idea where she was staying, only that it wasn't the Waterfront.

He dug through her pockets, hoping for a room key but found nothing. Then he spotted her purse he'd dumped next to her. He rummaged through it, but no hotel key and no cell phone. Just a handful of condoms. He couldn't help grinning. That little horny devil. Then he remembered just how unnecessary they were and winced.

When he found her black wallet, he flipped it open to her driver's license. Cute photo. He smiled briefly, admiring her impish grin when he realized there was something funny about her license. It was a Washington license, not an Arizona license.

Finn frowned and pulled it out. Definitely a photo of Ronnie, but the rest of it looked like something a kid would make in arts and crafts. The worst fake ID Finn had ever seen.

He shook his head, chuckling, then saw something had dropped onto the ground when he'd pulled out the fake ID from her wallet. An Arizona license, her real ID, he figured. She lived in Phoenix, on Cherry Street, hence the porn name. Her middle name was Alison. Her birthday…

Finn did some mental calculations and after he did the math three times, his entire body went cold. She wasn't even eighteen yet.

Finn dropped her wallet in horror.

"Omigod." He stood up, his hand covering his mouth, and quickly scanned the area for anyone watching him. A couple stragglers wandering around the marina, but nobody seemed to be paying him any attention. He bent down and stuffed the IDs back into her purse, his heart beating out of his chest.

This wasn't happening. He could not, absolutely could *not,* risk being associated with a minor. He was the general manager of one of the most successful restaurants in Redondo Beach—hell, all of the South Bay. She could invent whatever she wanted about him. Accuse him of sexual assault. Especially because he'd disappointed her. She would probably hold a grudge. His life would be over.

He knew what he had to do. He left Ronnie there on the grass and stumbled back to the Ferrari. After managing to get the key into the ignition after the fourth try, he peeled out of there. He felt a jolt followed by an awful scraping sound. Shit. Finn jumped out of the car and saw that he had sideswiped a black pickup.

He peered at Porter's sports car but didn't notice anything. Maybe a slight scrape on the driver's side door. He checked the pickup and thought he saw a dent but couldn't be positive. The truck was a piece of crap anyway, it was covered in dings and scratches. The owner probably wouldn't even notice. Finn hopped back into the Ferrari.

On the drive back, he mulled over his next step.

He'd go home and call—call who? Porter? Nine-one-one? Finn shook his head. His thoughts kept flitting around and around; he couldn't focus. He just had to get some sleep and figure it out later.

FIVE

Finn woke early the next morning with a pounding headache and it felt like a small furry animal had died in his mouth. He wondered why he was freezing, then realized he was still in Porter's car with the top down. Apparently, he'd parked on the street outside of his place last night and passed out. Wasn't the first time. He leaned back in the seat, closed his eyes, and groaned.

My god, what the hell did he do last night? How did he get such a monstrous hangover? What did he drink and—oh fuck. Finn opened his eyes and sat up.

Ronnie. He'd left her at the marina. He had to go get her.

Finn stiffly extricated himself from the car and shuffled inside his building, thankful his neighbors weren't early risers. They were all young kids in their twenties who partied into the wee hours. Climbing the stairs to the second floor, he clutched his throbbing head as he made his way into his apartment. He downed some aspirin and Gatorade, eyeing his cell phone on the counter top. He picked it up and saw he had about a dozen text messages and voicemails from Porter. Probably checking to make sure everything was okay. Well, he was going to have to wait.

He showered and put Visine in his bloodshot eyes, felt human again. Almost. Finn took a deep breath and glanced at his cell phone. Seven-ten. He had less than an hour until he was due at the restaurant. No problem.

He went back outside and headed to his beat-up Saab parked half a block away. He stopped. Screw that. He was taking the Ferrari.

Before he climbed inside, he noticed a long scrape on the driver's side door reminding him of last night's little fender bender. More of a scratch rather than a dent. Nothing a little toothpaste wouldn't take off.

Traffic was light since it was not even 8 a.m. yet and he made it to King Harbor in a record fif-teen minutes. When he pulled into the same spot he parked in last night, he noted the black pickup was gone. Thank god. He was in no mood to see another reminder of how fucked up he was last night.

He jogged down to the grassy area where he had left Ronnie, wincing at the jackhammer in his head with each bounce, stopped cold when he arrived at the spot. She was gone.

Shit. Finn looked around the marina, hoping he'd screwed up and this wasn't the right spot. But it was. The Moonshine was down gangway fifteen, directly in front of him, and this was the grassy place she conked out.

"Fuck, fuck, fuck," he muttered, running his hand through his hair. After circling the entire harbor, checking all the shrubbery in case she crawled into it to sleep off the booze, he deduced that she and her big black handbag had vanished.

He took a deep breath and turned around, heading back to the Ferrari. Time to go to work. Nothing else that could be done here. He'd figure out what to do later.

But when Finn spotted Porter storming through the parking lot toward his restaurant around eleven-thirty, he still hadn't come up with a plan. Unless you counted praying that Ronnie was safe and nobody saw them together as a plan. Then he had a rock solid one.

"What's up, man?" Finn grinned.

"Your office," Porter growled, grabbing Finn's arm.

"I'll meet you in there." Finn tried to yank his arm back. "I'm in the middle of a busy lunch rush here."

"Finn, I don't give a shit about your lunch rush," Porter said through gritted teeth.

Finn knew he had to talk to him right that second.

"Okay." Finn walked back to his office, Porter hot on his heels. When he entered his door code for his office, Porter practically flung him inside like a bouncer tossing a drunk into the street.

"Sit," Porter commanded. He closed the door and glowered at Finn. They were roughly the same height, same build even, but Finn felt small. He slunk into his chair.

"I don't know what's wrong with you, man," Porter began. "I just don't understand. I really don't."

Finn studied his hands, feeling like a child in the principal's office. He tried to look nonchalant. "Look, I can explain."

"Please do." Porter paused. "I'd love to hear your reason for why my boat looks like thirty high school kids partied on it and all my vintage wines are gone."

Finn opened his mouth but nothing came out.

"I swear I told you not to touch any of my booze

or am I crazy? Did I imagine that?" Porter raised his hands up in the air, a flabbergasted look on his face. "Was I speaking English?"

"I'm sorry," Finn cried. "That girl—she was a total lush, man! I mean, she just drank and opened bottle after bottle. She was out of control."

Porter shook his head and blew air out of his mouth. "I had to clean up that whole mess. I was late to work. And that whole time, I kept thinking, what is Finn doing? Does he just not care?"

Finn inhaled, ready to tell him about the girl. Her age, how he lost her. Probably a bad time, but shit, he had to say something. And it was weighing down on him like an anchor. "Porter, I think you should know—"

Porter held up his hand. "I'm not done." He hesitated as if gauging his thoughts. "You're like a brother to me, Finn. We've known each other how long?"

Finn cleared his throat. "Twenty-eight years," he said softly.

"Twenty-eight years." Porter paused. "We've been through *a lot*, Finn."

Finn waited, a sickening feeling growing in his gut.

"And I know you'd do anything for me," Porter continued. "Shit, you proved that already."

Finn met Porter's eyes. He felt himself nodding.

"I think about it every day. How I would have none of this if it weren't for what you did." He sighed. "But it's got to stop, man. No more boat. And no more Ferrari. You're on your own with your love trysts and hook-ups or whatever. I'm done."

Finn nodded. Okay, he figured that was coming. It sucked and he knew it would put a major cramp on his love life but so be it. He deserved it. At least he still had the use of the hotel rooms.

"It's for your own good, Finn." Porter turned, opening the office door. He spotted his yacht cap on Finn's desk and snatched it up, putting it on his head.

"We still on for the game tonight? Shark's Cove?" Finn asked in a small voice.

Porter paused in the doorway, an uncomfortable silence filling the cramped room. Loud voices and laughter rang outside, but at that moment, all Finn could hear was that dead quiet.

"I don't think so, dude," his friend finally said, his back still turned to him. "I don't think it's a good idea."

Panic seized Finn's throat. "What—what do you mean?"

"I don't think you should call me for a while."

"What? What are you talking about?" Finn leaped up and grabbed Porter's shoulder, wrenching him around. "I'm sorry, man. I told you," he begged. "I'll never do it again. I swear."

The look of pity in Porter's eyes shut Finn up. "You don't get it, do you? You're a mess. You need to clean up your fucking life, man."

He walked out, slamming the door behind him. Finn sagged against his desk, feeling worse than he'd ever felt after any break up.

SIX

The fight with Porter certainly didn't help Finn's predicament. Not only was he unable to sleep or breathe without thinking of Ronnie but now he had the loss of his best friend to make his life that much more unbearable. Even though he knew Porter would have been shocked at what Finn did to the poor girl, at the very least, he would have had a good idea of what to do next.

The next few days following Ronnie's disappearance and the blowout with Porter, Finn perused the local papers for stories about a missing girl. Nothing. He watched the news every night with knots in his stomach until he thought he was going to puke. No mention of a missing tourist. Every time his cell phone rang he prayed it was Ronnie, saying she was fine, but it was always work related. Finn was also hoping Porter would call or text but he was giving him the silent treatment. Finn sent text after text apologizing but received nothing in return.

By the fourth day, Finn felt his insides starting to unclench. He even wandered down to the harbor, spotting the Moonshine but not daring to board it in case Porter installed motion security cameras. He wasn't sure what he was looking for but thought it was worth a shot to see if anything new turned up. It was the same grassy area at the end of gangway fifteen. No body or purse to be found.

Was everything going to be okay? Finn didn't want to assume that, but it seemed like there was a good chance that this was all just going to blow over.

Until the moment Marisa mentioned the missing girl and he watched the news report on Ronnie. Now the real nightmare began.

SEVEN

The clanging noises from the arcade jolted Finn from his thoughts of the past five days. He had to return to the restaurant, explain his sudden departure to Courtney, the evening manager. The uptight bitch would surely be wondering where the hell he'd disappeared to. He told Emily he'd be right back, and he'd been gone almost forty minutes. Shit.

Hurrying back along the pier, his footsteps echoed on the wooden boardwalk. His anxiety over Ronnie swirled around in his head like the churning tide below. Screaming kids ran past him in shorts and tank tops. Tourists speaking a foreign language he didn't recognize walked by wearing fanny packs and sturdy Teva sandals.

I'm just going to play it cool, act like nothing happened, he thought. She was just a regular customer who had lunch. *A cute kid, right? Yeah, I think I remember her.* Sure he chatted with her during lunch, but he did that with everyone. Lord knows his staff was used to him plopping down next to customers, okay beautiful women, and hanging out there for a while. It would be nothing unusual.

The big problem was Finn's business card. He gave Ronnie one with his cell phone number on the back. That might look a little suspicious. Surely the cops would search her room and find it, right? Unless she threw it away. He prayed she tossed it. Or maybe it disappeared with her handbag. That'd be lucky.

His other concern was Tomas who served her. Did he overhear Finn ask her out? The thought of his sullen, oafish bartender pissed him off. If it wasn't for him, Finn wouldn't even *be* in this situation. The guy obviously wouldn't know a fake ID if it kicked him in the balls. Or he probably did and just didn't give a shit.

When he returned to the restaurant and pushed his way through the glass doors, the rush of cool air conditioning enveloped him. Aaaah, that was better. Putting his jacket back on, he noticed Emily and his PM host, Lisa, standing together behind the host stand, giggling and looking at their phones. Emily wasn't even in her uniform. She had taken the black restaurant vest off and her tits were practically begging to be released from her tight white top.

He stood directly in front of his two hostesses. They ignored him. They were on Facebook because Lisa said, "Why would that loser friend me?" Good god. He cleared his throat. They still didn't notice him. Finn admired Emily's cleavage for a little bit longer and then said, "Ahem!" They both looked up at that moment and Lisa turned red. She stashed her phone inside the host stand compartment and smiled.

"Hi, Mr. Roose." Lisa wasn't bad-looking for a Chinese or Japanese girl or whatever she was. Finn had never been a chow mein chaser. Maybe it was because their boobs were always so small. "Sorry we were just—"

Emily interrupted her, looking excited. "Courtney's talking to the police."

Finn froze. "What? What police?" Oh god, it was starting already. He figured he had a couple days before they'd show up here. He felt the sweat pool underneath his arms and on his upper lip.

"The Redondo Beach Police," Lisa chimed in. "We think they're here about that missing girl."

Emily nodded. "Totally."

Finn's head throbbed. He scanned the fairly empty restaurant. Only a few people were there finishing up a late lunch or coming in for an early happy hour. "Where?"

"In the office," Lisa said.

"Oh, here they come," Emily squealed.

Finn looked where she was pointing and saw Courtney, her blonde hair piled on top of her head in a severe bun, with two men in suits, one an older Asian male and the other a baby-faced surfer-looking kid. Detectives. Heading straight for him. Courtney looked grim and the detectives weren't smiling either. Crap. Finn gulped and hoped he didn't look as guilty as he felt. He plastered a smile on his face but not before he wiped the sweat off his upper lip.

"How are we all doing today?" Finn said.

Courtney ignored him. The detectives eyeballed him without saying anything.

"Can I get my tip money now?" Emily asked.

Courtney nodded at Emily and gestured for her to follow her to the back of the restaurant. She glanced back at Finn and said, "These detectives would like a word with you, Finn." Then she turned and stalked away with Emily hot on her heels.

"Okay, what can I do for you, gentlemen?" Finn gestured to a nearby empty booth to sit down but the two detectives didn't budge.

"Are you Phineas Roose?" the Asian detective asked.

"Yes." Finn smiled.

"I'm Detective Wu and this is Detective Pierce." The Asian man gestured to himself and his baby-faced partner. "We want to ask you a few questions."

Finn nodded. He wanted desperately to take his jacket off but was afraid his shirt would have sweat stains under his arms. God, did someone turn the heat on or something?

"Okay, uh..." Finn looked around for a quiet place to chat but there were servers doing roll-ups in the far corner of the restaurant, which was closed now until dinner started. "How about the office then?"

They nodded and waited for Finn to lead the way. He turned and felt every pair of eyes in the restaurant watching him. Thank god the lunch rush was over but it didn't do much to relieve his pin-balling nerves. He led the cops past the kitchen. Two dishwashers, Roberto and Jose, ducked their heads down when Finn caught them staring.

He turned the corner and almost smacked into Courtney and Emily.

"The office is all yours," Courtney said. She didn't even look at him.

Finn nodded. Courtney and Emily hurried away. He walked into his office and waited for the detectives to shuffle in before shutting the door. He perched on the edge of his desk like he had somewhere to go and would need to take off any second. At least that's the impression he was trying to give.

Detective Wu wasn't buying it. "Please, sit down, Mr. Roose." He pointed to Finn's swivel chair.

He hesitated but figured it wasn't worth arguing about. He sat and said, "What's this about? I'm late for an appointment." Hopefully they wouldn't ask him where or what because he hadn't the slightest idea.

"You'll get to your appointment," Detective Pierce said.

"Do you know why we're here, Mr. Roose?" Detective Wu towered over Finn in his little chair which he knew was exactly why he was sitting in it.

Finn thought quickly. Should he assume it's for Ronnie or should he just play dumb? He tried to calculate which approach made him look guiltier. He decided an innocent person would be eager to gossip about a missing tourist, just like Lisa and Emily were. Redondo Beach didn't get much excitement other than blue whale sightings. "Is it about that missing girl?"

"What makes you think that?" Detective Pierce jumped in, puffing his chest out.

Finn wondered which one was the good cop since they both seemed to hate him. "Well, it's all over the news, isn't it? She stayed around here apparently so..." He shrugged.

"Yes, we're here about Rhonda Alison Havemeyer," Detective Wu said. "Did she come in to your restaurant?"

Finn noticed the Asian detective had an annoying habit of fussing with his gun belt. He kept hiking it up and drumming his fingers on it. Finn caught himself staring at the gun in his holster. "Umm...I think so." He pretended to look thoughtful. "I saw her picture on the news. Cute girl." Finn nodded. "She looks familiar so she probably did. We're one of the more popular restaurants in Redondo Beach." He smiled.

"Did you talk to her?" Detective Wu didn't return the smile.

Finn shrugged. "I don't recall. Like I said, I'm not even positive she came into the restaurant."

The detectives glanced at each other. Detective Pierce cleared his throat. "You don't remember giving her your business card, for example?"

Finn did his thoughtful face again. "I may have. I do give out my business cards quite often." He paused. "I am the general manager here so I try to make face time with as many guests as possible." Might as well remind them how important he was around here.

"Do all your business cards have your cell phone number written on the back?" Detective Pierce asked with a knowing smirk.

Finn swallowed. Shit, it was just as he feared. They must have searched her hotel room and found his card. He hadn't thought of a plausible reason yet. "Well, some do." *Think, think, think.* Finn spoke slowly, stalling for time. Then he had it. "I like guests to feel welcome. The personal touch, you know?" He smiled, leaned back in his chair.

The two men traded looks again. Finn wished they would stop doing that.

"Giving out your cell phone number is quite the personal touch, Mr. Roose. Is this a common practice among restaurant GMs?" Detective Pierce had that smirk again.

Finn tried to appear calm. He knew it sounded lame, but shit, this was what he was going with. "Well, as you may know or not know, tourists are quite common in this restaurant since we're part of a hotel. They often ask me where a good place is to rent bikes or go whale-watching." Finn paused. "I'm happy to give them my opinion. I do know the area rather well and have contacts all over, of course." He gave them a wide smile, hoping he appeared charming and popular.

The two detectives remained stoic, watching him.

"So sometimes I provide them with my personal cell phone number in case they'd like last-minute reservations somewhere and want me to pull some strings." He shrugged. "It's no bother to me and it's much easier than tracking me down through my restaurant here."

The two men seemed to be processing this.

"The personal touch," Finn said. He wished he would just stop talking.

"Uh-huh," Detective Wu said finally. His beady eyes narrowed even more at him. "And are pretty young girls the usual recipients of this personal touch?"

Finn shrugged again. "Whoever seems interested in getting hooked up with last minute reservations somewhere or getting VIP treatment at a club." He pretended to pick some lint off his pants, hoping he looked disinterested in the entire conversation. "It's usually the families or groups of girls traveling together. It varies, to be honest."

"So you don't remember exactly if you gave Rhonda Havemeyer your business card with your personal cell phone number on it or not." Detective Wu hitched up his gun belt again.

Finn shook his head. "Like I said, I may have. I just honestly don't recall."

"You didn't visit her hotel room or meet her at her hotel?" Detective Wu asked.

Finn shook his head. "I don't even recall if I met her or not, let alone go to her hotel room." He waited. "What hotel was she staying at?" Finn was honestly curious.

"Why, what hotel did you see her at?" Detective Pierce interjected.

"I didn't see her at any hotel." Finn was getting annoyed with this interrogation. They obviously had nothing on him other than finding his business card in her hotel room and now they were fishing.

Muted laughter broke out in the hallway behind the closed office door. Then he heard a knock. Nobody budged. Detective Pierce was closest to the door and finally opened it. It was John, his PM bartender. At the sight of the two detectives, his eyes widened.

"Oh, sorry, Finn." He glanced back and forth between Finn and the two men. "I—I thought... well, never mind."

"What is it, John?" Finn was welcome for any interruption. "You need something?"

John hesitated. "Uh—it's okay. Well, yeah. I just needed a comp. They're ready to leave and—"

"Where's Courtney?" Finn asked.

"Outside with corporate."

Crap. Finn forgot about corporate showing up tonight. He was supposed to be the one schmoozing them which meant kissing their fat asses and laughing at their inappropriate jokes. Which meant he needed to stick around tonight while Courtney managed the restaurant. He sighed. Better than staying at home, wringing his hands and waiting for the cops to bust his door down.

The detectives seemed to realize the interview was over. They didn't look too happy about it.

Finn stood up and said, "If you excuse me, I have a restaurant to run. Please let me know if I can be of any more help."

It wasn't until he walked the detectives to the front of the restaurant and watched them swagger through the parking lot that Finn finally took a breath without feeling the urge to throw up.

EIGHT

Still no sign of Ronnie two days later. Finn watched the news and followed her story, the knot in his gut loosening with each passing day. Detectives Wu and Pierce didn't come into his restaurant again so Finn assumed they were satisfied with his lame story. For the moment, at least.

Or maybe it was that the innocent Rhonda Alison Havemeyer was not so innocent after all. The Redondo Beach police investigation turned up quite a few interesting tidbits.

For starters, it turned out she had been staying at the Falcon Inn, a clean but rundown motel with peeling orange paint and a missing letter on the sign so it actually read "Falco Inn." The motel was on Pacific Coast Highway, a couple miles north of the Redondo Beach Pier next to a vacant Blockbuster and a dive bar called Bud's. Finn wondered why a cute young girl would stay at such a sad motel all by herself.

Ronnie's parents were just as mystified as Finn. When they made the trip out to the South Bay from Arizona to join in the search for their missing daughter and beg on camera for any information, they insisted they had no idea what kind of hotel she had been staying at.

"We never would have allowed this," her father growled in one interview.

"She told me you could hear the ocean at night," Ronnie's tearful mother added.

Finn knew the only thing you could hear from the Falcon Inn was the incessant traffic on PCH, the drunks shouting obscenities as they stumbled out of Bud's, and vagrants rummaging around the dumpster on the side of the motel. He'd stayed there a couple times when he'd been in a pinch and needed a room after scoring a drunken chick at Bud's.

Things became even weirder when the parents revealed that Ronnie was supposed to be attending some kind of week-long Christian retreat in Redondo Beach. Imagine their horror when they learned there was no such retreat. Finn felt bad for her parents who looked more and more like clueless saps. These poor people had no idea what their daughter was doing or who she was doing it with.

Apparently, Ronnie had been to Bud's once. Or

at least tried to. The bouncer said he refused to let her in because her ID was obviously fake—he didn't care how low-cut her shirt was.

The media spun this into a tale of a rebellious runaway, not a missing young woman. The police seemed satisfied with this conclusion, saying there was no indication of foul play, and Finn had no problem with it either.

Ronnie's parents, however, didn't accept it and hired a private investigator to look into their daughter's disappearance when they realized the Redondo Beach Police Department had all but closed their file.

Finn scoffed when he heard this. A private investigator, please. Ronnie's parents didn't look like they had much money. Finn figured the guy would poke around for a couple days, then give up when the parents couldn't pay him.

He wasn't worried about this private investigator in the slightest.

NINE

Finn still wasn't worried when the private investigator came into the restaurant. His name was Jackson; Finn wasn't sure if that was his first or his last name. He appeared to be in his late forties, early fifties even, and was quite small, five-seven at the most, but he looked solid. Like he could pack a punch and not be shy about it.

He told Jackson the exact same thing he told the detectives, that he probably gave her his business card, but he did that with many of his guests. The P.I. didn't say much. He just nodded his balding head and scanned Finn's office like he was memorizing every detail. When Finn escorted him to the glass doors leading out to the parking lot, he noticed Jackson scan the restaurant in the same manner.

"I am so sorry I couldn't be of more help, Mr.—er, Jackson," Finn said. "Please do come back in for lunch sometime soon, won't you?"

"Where did Ronnie sit when she came in?" Jackson asked.

The question threw Finn off. Without thinking, he glanced over at the bar where she had sat nursing her glass of wine almost two weeks ago, then realized his mistake. He scanned the restaurant, pretending to search for someone. He smiled at the P.I., hoping his face wasn't as flushed as it felt. "I'm sorry, I must take care of my closing server. She should be ready to cash out any minute. You know how it is, well, maybe you don't." Jesus, what was wrong with him? "If you will excuse me." Finn paused, not wanting to be rude, but he had to get the hell away from this guy before he said something really stupid.

Jackson gazed at him, his black eyes revealing nothing, then finally nodded. He wordlessly handed Finn his business card before exiting the restaurant.

Finn watched the P.I. walk carefully through the parking lot like he was inspecting the asphalt for cracks. Anxiety crawled through Finn like a spider. He hoped he never saw that little man again.

Finn glanced at the card in his hand and read, "Jackson, Private Investigator" with a phone number underneath. The area code was six-oh-two which he figured was Phoenix. Finn crumpled up the card and tossed it into the trash.

TEN

A couple days later and with no further visits from the police or Jackson, Finn began to think he'd averted disaster. He was starting to feel like himself again for the first time since that awful night almost two weeks ago. He even decided he was ready for a hot date. Maybe that redhead would finally give him her number.

But he wanted to make amends with Porter first. It was killing him that his best friend refused to talk to him and now that the Ronnie fiasco seemed to have died down, Finn was ready to try again. He'd cry or grovel if he had to, he didn't care anymore.

Finn picked up the phone in his office to call Porter when he realized there was no dial tone. "Hello?" he asked after a few seconds.

"Oh, Mr. Roose, it's me, Emily," she said over the intercom. "That was weird. It didn't even buzz or anything."

"Yes, Emily, what is it?"

"You have a call."

"Who is it?"

"Uh, well he wouldn't say. But I think it's that same guy from like a week ago?"

Finn couldn't remember.

"You told me to take a message but he hung up before I could. He talks real soft."

Now Finn remembered. He'd been annoyed Emily interrupted him while he was working the redhead. The day he saw the news report on Ronnie. "Okay. Well, did you get his name this time and ask what he wanted?"

There was a pause. "Um, no. He just said it was important you speak to him."

"Fine." Finn couldn't imagine what was so important. "Line two?"

"Uh-huh."

He pressed the button for line two. "Hello, this is Finn Roose."

"Hello?" a soft voice answered. Finn had to strain to hear him. He sounded young, maybe early twenties. Husky too, like he had a cold or something.

"This is Finn Roose," he repeated, trying to sound pleasant. "Is there something I can help you with?"

A long pause. Finn knew the kid was still on the

line because he was breathing heavy. He was about to tell the guy to get his jollies off somewhere else when he finally spoke.

"I saw you. With the girl," the guy muttered. His voice was pretty muffled like he was talking away from the phone or something.

The hair stood up on Finn's neck. "Excuse me?"

"You heard me."

"I—I don't know what you're—what girl?" Finn asked. He licked his lips, felt like he had swallowed sand.

"Don't play stupid with me, man. Ronnie, I saw you with Ronnie," he said.

Was this a prank? Maybe it was the P.I. fucking with him? "Is this Jackson?"

"I don't know no fuckin' Jackson," the guy said. His voice became louder.

"Well, then who the hell are you?"

"That's not important, *esé*."

Mexican dude? He thought of his back of the house staff. He'd fired enough of them over the years to make enemies out of any of them. "I don't believe you."

"Oh yeah? You better believe me, man. Or you're going to be in serious trouble."

"Then where did you see us, huh?"

There was a pause, then, "The marina. King Harbor."

Shit. This kid wasn't kidding, but Finn kept playing the denial card. "I don't know what you're talking about."

"You think I'm making this shit up? I saw you, man. You fucking left her. Right there on the grass."

Okay, the guy obviously saw him. "Then you know I didn't do anything to her."

"Then *you* won't mind if I tell the cops what I saw, will you?"

Finn was silent.

"That's what I thought. I want five grand in cash. Maybe then I won't go to the cops."

Finn laughed. "You gotta be fucking kidding me. I don't have five grand, man. Who do you think I am?"

"I don't give a shit who you are. Just get it. Or I go to the cops and tell them everything I saw."

"How do I know you won't go to the cops anyway?"

"You don't. But you don't have much choice now, do you?"

Finn didn't have a response to that.

"Go to the liquor store on the corner of Crenshaw and Imperial. Park behind it and wait. Leave the doors unlocked."

Finn scribbled down "liquor store" and "Crenshaw and Imperial" on a post-it. "Behind liquor store, doors unlocked, okay. When?"

"Tonight. Eleven-thirty. With the cash."

"What do you look like?"

But the guy'd already hung up, the dial tone blaring in his ear. Finn stared at the post-it he wrote. Did that really just happen? He looked at the clock in his office. Four-thirty.

Finn sat back in his chair, unsure what to do. He felt paralyzed. Maybe he was in shock. Who the fuck was this guy? And how the hell was he going to get five grand in seven hours? He thought of Porter, but Porter wouldn't even talk to him.

Christ. He had about two hundred dollars in his checking account. Maybe a couple thousand in his savings. And that was it. No IRA or 401(k). He was fucked.

Finn groaned and leaned over, staring at the floor. Then he spotted the safe underneath his desk. Hello.

ELEVEN

Finn pulled into a rundown strip mall at the corner of Crenshaw and Imperial Highway at eleven-twenty. He found the liquor store the blackmailer told him about. The only one around, although there was a mini-mart next to a gas station across the street. He hoped the kid didn't mean that one.

Finn drove around to the back. There was an alley behind the store with a dumpster and trash scattered all around it. He really didn't like the idea of parking there. It was dark, the only dim light was from the front of the store. He could get easily trapped if someone parked in front and someone behind. What if the guy brought friends? He wished he had a gun or a knife even. Stupid of him not to bring *something*.

Should he park in the front of the store where it was safer even though the guy told him the back? Then again, how safe was Ingle-fucking-hood at eleven-thirty at night? Shit. No difference really. So

Finn sat in his car and waited. He stared at the clock on his dash. Eleven-twenty-five. He hoped the guy would be on time. This waiting around in the dark stressed him out. He checked and rechecked to make sure the doors were unlocked like the kid said. He didn't like that either. His instinct was to lock down his car like Fort Knox.

Finn thought about the five grand he stole from the restaurant safe and glanced down at the envelope holding the cash. Probably not a good idea to just leave it sitting on the passenger seat. He threw it into the glove compartment. He was going to have to sell his car or something to repay it. Maybe he could fake a robbery. He had a couple days before the next bank pickup. Then it'd probably be another week before someone noticed the discrepancy.

When the clock read eleven-forty, Finn started to get nervous. Was he in the right spot? Maybe he wrote the instructions down wrong. He did say Crenshaw and Imperial, right?

He was digging around for his scribbled notes when he heard the sound of his rear passenger door opening. Finn glanced in the rearview to see a guy wearing large dark sunglasses, a baseball cap, and a bandana tied around his mouth slide into the backseat. He looked like some bandito out of a bad movie.

"Are you—?"

"Shut up," the guy said. His voice was muffled because of the bandana.

Finn smelled a trace of pot and cheap cologne that made his stomach curdle. He attempted to turn around but something cold and metal stuck him in the back of the neck.

"Don't or I'll kill you." The voice was flat.

Finn froze, his heart seizing up in his chest. He'd never had a gun mashed against his head before. Sure, he'd been shot at once by a pissed-off husband, but that was from far away. It wasn't likely that this guy behind him would miss.

"Gimme the money."

The kid was hard to understand with that stupid bandana but Finn figured it out. He reached for the glove compartment and his blackmailer became agitated.

"Whoa, hold on there, man!" The gun pressed harder into Finn's neck, pushing his head down. "What you reaching for?" His voice jumped a couple octaves.

"Take it easy," Finn said. His voice shook and panic welled up in his gut. "I'm getting the money like you asked." He gestured to the glove compartment. "It's in there."

There was a pause and Finn listened to the traffic zooming by on Imperial Highway. He hoped a cop car would cruise by, then thought better of it. The police are what he did *not* want. That's why he was in this goddamn mess in the first place.

"Okay, go slow," the kid ordered, the flat dead tone returning. "Nothing funny, *esé*."

Finn slowly reached for the glove compartment again, feeling like he was moving underwater, and opened it. He grabbed the fat white envelope and shut the compartment.

"Okay, hand it over."

Finn passed the envelope back and it was snatched out of his hand. The gun was still pressed to the back of his neck as he heard paper rustling. He glanced in the rearview and saw the kid examining the envelope.

"Who are you?" Finn asked. He tried to figure out what the guy looked like but it was too dark.

No response.

"Why didn't you help Ronnie then if you saw us?" Finn continued to stare at the kid in the rearview, familiarity needling him.

"Maybe I did."

That threw Finn. "Huh? What do you mean?"

But it was too late. The guy was out of the car, disappearing with a slam of the door. Finn whipped his head around to check out the alley but it was too dark to see anything. Shit. Finn leaned back in his seat and exhaled. He'd been holding his breath the whole time.

Lights flooded his car causing Finn to practically leap out of his seat. Christ, were the cops here? Did the kid turn him in anyway? He looked around wildly, struggling to get his keys in the ignition. He heard a loud metal clanging, then realized it was just a liquor store employee, Indian or Pakistani, dumping out the trash. The man stared at Finn, suspicion clouding his features. Finn didn't need any encouragement. With shaking hands, he started the engine and got the hell out of there.

TWELVE

The next morning, Finn received a call as he was about to leave for work. The caller ID read "Porter" and Finn almost squealed with excitement. "Porter, it's you. I'm so glad you called. I've been—"

"Finn, I have to talk to you." Porter cut him off. "Now."

Finn frowned. Porter sounded stressed. "Sure, man, I'd like that." He grabbed his jacket and headed for the front door. "Tonight? Shark's Cove?"

"No, I need to see you right now."

"Um, well, I'm running late to work and have to head out." Finn grabbed his car keys and opened the front door.

"I'm fucking serious, man. I'm coming over right now."

Finn froze in the doorway. Porter rarely cursed.

"What's going on, Porter?"

"The Redondo Beach police want me to come in. For a chat."

Finn squeezed the car keys in his hand, the metal grooves digging into his palms. "What for?"

"I don't know. But I think it's about that missing girl."

"What? What makes you think that?" Why was his voice so high all of a sudden?

"Oh, I don't know, Finn. Maybe the fact that they asked if I owned a red Ferrari California that had been recently damaged. And if I had taken any young ladies out on my boat lately."

Finn swallowed.

"And the only time I had recent damage was that night you borrowed it. To take out your underage floozy."

Nobody used words like "floozy" except Porter. "I can explain. I was going to—"

"Christ, Finn, you *did* take that poor girl out. For god's sake, what the hell were you thinking?"

"I didn't know how old she was, man. I swear!"

"What did you do to her, Finn?"

"Nothing!" Finn leaned his forehead against the door jamb. His mind was a jumbled mess of questions. "What did you say? You didn't mention me, did you?"

"No, I didn't." Porter sighed. "God knows why I didn't."

Finn sagged with relief. "Thank you."

"Don't thank me." Porter's voice was hard again. "They want me to come in to the station right now. I've been out of town so they called me on my cell last night. Asked me all these crazy questions." A bitter-sounding laugh came out. "How did I know you'd be involved with this seventeen-year-old missing girl? God, it doesn't fucking surprise me, Finn."

Finn had never heard Porter curse this much. "I tried to tell you, man. I really wanted to tell you, but you were so mad and I—"

"They say it's only for an interview, but I'm not fucking stupid," Porter continued as if he didn't hear Finn. "They're going to arrest me, I'm sure of it. Unless I tell them the truth."

"No. No, wait, Porter. Hang on a sec, let's figure this out." His voice sounded whiny and desperate but he didn't care at this point. "We need to agree on what you're going to say."

"I'm telling the truth. You can come with me or you can just sit tight and wait for them to come knocking on your door." Porter paused. "It's up to you."

Finn was silent. No way in hell he was going to

the police with Porter. He just couldn't.

"Did you kill her, Finn? Tell me." Porter sounded like he was afraid of the answer.

"No!" Finn stormed back into his apartment, slamming the door. He needed a drink. A bourbon. Something. "I didn't do shit. She passed out and I—I left her there. On the grass right by the fifteen gangway." There. He said it. Despite his mounting panic, he felt better. He'd finally told someone what a dumbass jerk he was. He opened his cupboard but all he had was half a bottle of Bailey's Irish Cream.

Porter was quiet. Finn thought maybe he'd hung up but then he finally spoke. "I didn't think you were capable of killing anyone."

Finn nodded even though Porter couldn't see him. He grabbed the Bailey's and unscrewed the top with his right hand. He found a dirty glass in the sink and poured three fingers.

"You need to tell them the truth, Finn. I'm coming over right now to pick you up."

Finn slugged down half the drink and almost spat it out. God, that was disgusting. Maybe not the most appropriate choice for eight in the morning. "Wait a sec, man. Let's think about this."

"I'm not going down for something I didn't do."

There was a long heavy silence. Finn knew

Porter was thinking exactly what he was thinking. Because "going down for something I didn't do" was exactly what Finn had done for Porter sixteen years ago.

"Shit," Porter muttered.

Finn waited but he didn't say anything more. He slugged back the remainder of the liquor and almost gagged. He hated this creamy stuff, which is why it was the only booze left in his cupboard.

"I owe you a lot, Finn. But this—this is where it has to end."

He knew Porter was right but a part of him, a small cowardly part of him, was hoping his only friend would take the fall. It was a horrible thing to contemplate, and what kind of man was he if that's what he was hoping for?

But then we'd be even, Finn couldn't help thinking. Which was wrong in so many ways. They weren't sixteen anymore. At that age, you didn't have other people, loved ones, depending on you.

The sad thing was Finn still had nobody depending on him.

"I'll be at your house in twenty," Porter said quietly. "We're going in together."

Finn stared down into the grimy kitchen sink. Bits of food stuck to the stainless steel.

"Finn?"

He sighed. Shit. He had no choice. Time to clean it up, as Porter said.

"Okay?" Porter was beginning to sound impatient.

Finn wished he could just crawl into bed and make all this go away. "Okay," he managed. He felt nauseous.

"Good." Porter hung up.

Finn tossed his phone onto the kitchen counter and bolted for the bathroom where he threw up.

THIRTEEN

An hour went by and when Porter didn't show, Finn started to panic. He'd already called Courtney to let her know an emergency came up and he needed her to cover for him. She didn't sound too happy but reluctantly agreed. He thought about another shot of Bailey's but shoved that thought away when his stomach did a cartwheel.

After another fifteen minutes of staring out the window for Porter's car, Finn called his cell. No answer. When his voicemail came on, Finn said, "Porter, where the hell are you? I'm here…ready to go." He hung up.

Should he go to work or go to the police station? Christ. Finn paced back and forth on his threadbare carpet. If he left, Porter might show up and assume he chickened out and just head to the police station on his own. Finn wanted to be there while Porter was spilling his guts. Then again, maybe it was better not to be there.

"Shit!" He stared out the window for the hundredth time and still no Porter. Finn made a decision. He'd drive to Porter's house and if he wasn't there, he'd go to the police station and look for his car in the parking lot.

While he headed down Sepulveda Blvd. toward Manhattan Beach, Finn couldn't believe how many times he had to pull over to allow whizzing cop cars by. Then an ambulance. It wasn't until he turned down Porter's street that he began to feel like his stomach was sinking down a hole. A mess of black and whites, an ambulance, and even a fire engine at the end of the block. Finn drove slowly down the street, his curiosity turning into fear when he realized they were gathered around Porter's five-bedroom home.

He parked in someone's driveway and leaped out of the car. Curious neighbors stood outside watching the spectacle. Finn ran over only to be ordered back by a young kid who looked like he was playing cop.

"Sir, I need to ask you to step back."

"What happened?" Finn cried. "That's my best friend's house." He scanned the area wildly, looking for Porter. "Where's Porter?"

"Sir, I have to ask you to step back," the cop repeated.

There was a ruckus at the front door of Porter's house, and two paramedics emerged, pushing a gurney toward the waiting ambulance. Whoever was on the gurney was covered with a blood-soaked sheet. Porter's wife, Lana, stood near the ambulance back doors, weeping, her long blonde hair falling over her face. Finn ran over to her, dodging various onlookers.

"Lana."

She stared at Finn, tears streaming down, but her blue eyes were vacant, unseeing. She must be in shock, Finn thought.

"Lana? What happened?" Finn tried again. "Where's Porter?"

"Ma'am? Let's go." The paramedic was beside her now, one hand on her shoulder. "We have to go now."

A sob escaped from her and she nodded. The paramedic helped her into the back of the ambulance. He slammed the doors. Finn grabbed his arm.

"Please, tell me what happened."

The paramedic shook his head. "I'm sorry, sir." He pounded the back doors and then the young cop from earlier was in front of Finn, pushing him back. "Sir, you need to step away."

Finn watched as the ambulance pulled away from the curb. The squeal of the siren made him jump.

"That poor family," an older woman beside him clucked.

"Do you know what happened?"

The woman pointed to a Manhattan Beach police car that had a man sitting inside. The lights on top of the car whirled and it pulled away from the curb in the opposite direction of the ambulance. Finn tried to see who was sitting in the back seat, but they took off too quickly.

"That guy shot Lana's husband."

Finn wasn't sure he heard her right. "What?"

"That man shot Lana's husband," she repeated. "Just a little bit ago. I heard the gunshot from inside my house." She waved her hand to indicate where she lived.

Finn felt like he was going to puke again. He could still taste the Bailey's from earlier which wasn't helping.

"Who was that guy? Who shot him?"

She shrugged. "Some crazy man. I don't know what's happening to people these days."

"Everyone go home." The young cop waved his arms. "This is a crime scene. Everyone go home."

Finn staggered back to his Saab, about to climb inside, when he spotted a man watching him. He did a double take. It was that private investigator. Jackson.

They locked eyes until Finn finally looked away. The guy didn't move; he was like a statue. Angst washed over Finn as he climbed inside his car, cranking the engine. He glanced back at the little man in his rearview still watching him. What the fuck was he doing here? Finn backed out of the driveway and gunned it down the street, those black eyes boring into his skull.

FOURTEEN

It was all in the paper the next day. Ronnie's dad had shot Porter who was already dead by the time he arrived at the ER. Somehow he found out that Porter was wanted for questioning and decided to conduct his own form of justice by driving over to Porter's house and shooting him in the chest.

The Redondo Beach police had resumed their interest in Ronnie's case when a USC student called them with new information. He recognized the girl, claiming he saw her climb into a red convertible Ferrari with a tall guy sitting in the driver's seat a couple weeks ago while he was partying at the Hermosa Beach Pier. She'd told him she was going on a boat ride. The kid only saw the back of the driver's head, but he remembered the guy was wearing a black cap.

That set everything into motion. The cops tracked down owners of the very few red convertible Ferraris in the South Bay. A hit and run report in the parking lot of the King Harbor involving a red car on that same night led the police to narrow their search to King Harbor. The Redondo Beach police cross-checked their databases and found one owner of a red, convertible 2012 Ferrari California who was also the proud owner of a forty-four-foot sailboat called the Moonshine. Which happened to be docked in King Harbor.

The media lambasted Porter as a pervert and murderer. Talk around town and the internet was just as judgmental. How shocked everyone was that such a devoted father and hard-working entertainment lawyer could be caught up in something so sordid.

Finn wanted to scream at all these people. If only they knew the truth. Of course, one surefire way to reveal the truth was to go to the police station and turn himself in. Like he had intended to do. But something—something twisted and cowardly and ugly stopped him. It made him sick and he even came down with an awful flu that prevented him from going into work for a couple days. Which was torture because all he did was sit home and read the latest on his best friend.

Finn wanted to call Lana and offer his condolences but was too afraid. She was never a big fan of his and probably blamed him for all this. According to the media, she'd refused to comment. However, her friends and co-workers had no problem offering their take on things. How Porter would allegedly work late into the night, often coming home after Lana was already asleep. How the poor woman would complain she never saw him and little did she know he was out trolling around for young girls to seduce on his boat.

The police had confiscated the Moonshine as well as the Ferrari which Porter had already repaired. When Finn heard this he felt relief then panic. Can you still find DNA evidence in a newly repaired, recently cleaned vehicle? Can't they extrapolate DNA from almost anything these days? What if he left a strand of his hair or fingerprints aboard the Moonshine? His only hope was that Porter did such a good job of hosing the boat down that the cops would turn up nothing.

There was a memorial service for Porter a week later that Finn debated attending, but decided to go at the last minute. He was one of the last ones to arrive and sat way in the back. It was a sad service with plenty of weeping and nose-blowing. Many of Lana's friends and family were there and Finn recognized Porter's parents.

He was the first one to exit the church after the service. A Channel Nine news van was out front but other than that, the church grounds were quiet. Finn took a deep breath and closed his eyes, trying to relax. Didn't work. He still felt like a slimy schmuck for letting his best friend die in shame. The guilt was growing steadily like a malignant tumor. Right in the center of his chest.

People finally started to stream out of the church and Finn lingered, waiting for Lana. Dylan, Porter and Lana's five-year-old son, came out by himself and plopped down on the church steps. He doodled in the dirt with his finger. Lana followed but was too busy greeting people and nodding solemnly to pay much attention to him. Dylan looked so forlorn with his stiff black suit that Finn walked over and awkwardly lowered himself right next to him.

"Hey, buddy."

Dylan glanced at him, then went back to drawing circles in the dirt.

"You remember me?"

Dylan shrugged. Finn wouldn't be surprised if the kid had no idea who he was. He rarely went over to Porter's place because—well, because Porter never invited him. The thought made Finn sad. Was his friend embarrassed of him? Or maybe Porter just never had a reason to invite him. He was always working.

"Last time I saw you..." Finn paused and had to

think about it. Jesus, was it a couple years ago? No wonder the boy didn't know who the hell he was. He was only three. "It was your birthday party. You had Elmo there, remember?"

Dylan nodded. Maybe he smiled too. "I had an Elmo birthday cake too."

Finn grinned. "Yup, you sure did. Chocolate with red frosting."

Dylan definitely smiled that time. He peered at Finn shyly. Finn swallowed. The boy had Porter's long dark eyelashes, like a girl's. He felt tears welling in his eyes and brushed them away.

"Are you friends with my daddy?"

Finn nodded. He started drawing a circle with his finger so it intersected with Dylan's. Like one of those Venn diagrams that you learn in school but have no clue what the hell they're for.

"Is he—is he up in heaven?"

Finn looked at Dylan's hopeful face and beautiful thick lashes and wanted to hug him. He'd never wanted to do anything to a kid except smack them across the face or yell at them. Finn cleared his throat and patted Dylan's knee. "Yeah, kid, he's up in heaven. Looking down at us right now."

Dylan seemed worried. "Are you sure?"

"Of course I'm sure."

"But—but the kids at school say he's not. That

he's a—"

Finn waited but Dylan was done. It pissed Finn off that kids would say anything to this poor boy other than "I'm sorry."

"Honey?"

They both looked up to see Lana towering over them. She hesitated at the sight of Finn with her son, a slight frown on her carefully made-up face. Maybe wondering if she should be a bitch to Finn in front of Dylan. Finn stood up and smiled apologetically.

"Sorry, we were just drawing in the dirt."

She glanced down at the circles in the dirt, then held out her hand. "Honey, we have to go."

"I'm so sorry, Lana," Finn blurted. "I—I just want to say that I'm sorry." The tears started again and he wiped them away, feeling like an idiot.

Instead of ignoring him or glaring at him like he expected, she just bit her lip and nodded. She reached down and grabbed Dylan's hand, pulling him up. They walked down the steps toward an awaiting limo with guys dressed like they were in the Secret Service or something holding the media at bay. To Finn's surprise, Dylan turned around and waved at him. Finn waved back and decided it was time to man up and turn himself in. The kid deserved that much.

FIFTEEN

Of course, there was no rush, right? The police weren't going anywhere. Would it really matter if he turned himself in now versus a week from now? He didn't think so. Come to think of it, as he did a couple of days later, did he really need to turn himself in at all? The cops had surely closed their file and wouldn't be too thrilled with more paperwork.

Yet that nagging feeling wouldn't go away. *Turn yourself in.* The little voice in his head wouldn't shut up. He wished he'd never gone to the funeral and seen that kid.

The guilt was seriously screwing with his head because he wasn't even turned on by big titties anymore. The redhead was in the other day—the one he'd been after for over two months—and she finally gave Finn her number. The one time he didn't ask for it. Her name was Sharla and she was a massage therapist. Instead of promising to call her, he'd merely pocketed the number and muttered something about being busy. What the hell was wrong with him? She was a fucking massage therapist! Some other Finn had taken over and he really didn't like this guy at all. He was morose, anxious, and worst of all he didn't even want to get laid.

And he had another big problem. Corporate had contacted him about the missing five K. Did he have any idea what happened? They were having an auditor look into it and wanted copies of last month's financials. They assured him it was probably just a glitch but they needed to investigate. Finn agreed to help with whatever they needed and figured this allowed him a couple more weeks to come up with a plan. He needed it. So far, he wasn't having too much success.

Porter was right. He was a fucking mess. Always was and always would be.

The one time he didn't have any regrets was that day many years ago with Porter. The day that changed their lives forever.

SIXTEEN

It was their high school graduation night. Finn and Porter were leaving one party and heading to another. The sunroof was open as it was a typical balmy summer night in Orange County. Porter drove Finn's car that night because—well, because Finn as usual was hammered. He knew Porter was in pretty bad shape too, but at least he wasn't singing "Livin' La Vida Loca" at the top of his lungs.

Finn knew they were on borrowed time because in three months Porter would head off to Yale on a full scholarship, while Finn would attend Cypress Community College. Not exactly what Finn's dad had hoped for and he was still aggressively campaigning for his son to get into Pepperdine with a fast track to law school. That he had no desire to go to Pepperdine or study law wasn't even a factor to his dad.

Porter veered right, cutting through a strip mall

parking lot at eighty miles an hour. No cars in the lot because everything was closed. Porter swerved left and Finn practically smacked his head on the passenger window.

"Dude, what the fuck?" Finn cried. "You *that* drunk or what?"

"The shopping cart." Porter pointed and Finn spotted the glinting steel of a shopping cart. He was about to say 'good job' when he realized the SUV was still spinning and holy shit, was it actually tipping?

"Fuck, fuck, fuck," Porter muttered, cranking the wheel to straighten it out but the big gas guzzler wasn't cooperating. It rolled over and skidded on its right side, heading straight for the line of storefront windows. Porter screamed, metal scraped, and there was noise all around him. They hurtled toward Premiere Video and Finn thought he saw sparks shooting out.

He conked his head on something and there was a loud *smash* as they careened right through the front of the video store. Something like one of those balloon balls punched him in the face, momentarily blocking his vision, and he realized it was the air bag. The SUV slammed into something big. More loud noises and then silence. Dark in the store except for a faint light coming from somewhere in back.

"Holy fuck," Finn said. He was still in his seat, thankfully buckled in, but was lying on his right side. The windshield had cracked into a million little pieces like an intricate spider's web but amazingly remained intact. His entire body hurt and something wet dripped down his forehead. He heard moaning and realized Porter dangled above him.

"Porter, you okay?"

Porter coughed and moaned again. "Yeah, I think so."

"We've got to get out of the car." Finn thought he smelled gas or maybe that was just his imagination but he sure as shit didn't want to stick around to find out.

"My leg won't move." Porter screamed out in anguish.

Finn managed to undo the seatbelt. He couldn't get out of his door because the ground was directly underneath him. Then he realized the sun roof was open. He wormed his way out of the opening. He was pretty slim but it was still a tight squeeze. Every part of his body screamed in pain. He popped out like a newborn and tumbled down to the carpeted floor of the store with a groan. Oddly enough, he didn't feel as drunk as he had earlier. The adrenaline probably sobered him up.

"Hang on, Porter." Finn spotted a piece of wooden furniture, maybe part of a shelf, and grabbed it, holding it like a baseball bat. He heard sirens in the distance. He swung and smashed the cracked windshield and kept smashing until it shattered into little pebble pieces everywhere.

Porter managed to get his seatbelt off. He started to move forward toward Finn but howled in pain. "Shit, my leg, man."

"You have to keep moving." Finn reached through the gaping hole where the windshield used to be and tugged on Porter. "Come on, dude. You can't stay in there."

Porter inched forward but winced. "I must have broken it."

But Finn didn't give a shit if Porter's leg was missing. "The car is going to blow up, man. You have to get out of the fucking car!"

That did it. Porter heaved himself forward, shrieking at the top of his lungs, and Finn grabbed his arms, yanking him out of the car. They tumbled onto the carpet and lay there, breathing heavily and moaning. VHS tapes were scattered all over the floor around them. *Boogie Nights* was right by his head. Finn loved that movie.

Porter sniffed the air. "Is that gas?"

"Fuck!" They both scrambled up and Porter winced but didn't scream this time. Finn swung Porter's arm around his shoulders and half-dragged, half-carried him, crunching on glass. They stumbled through the front of the store, which was now a mangled mess of twisted steel and window shards.

"Hurry." Finn dragged his friend through the parking lot, praying they didn't hear an explosion behind them. They weren't far enough away yet.

"Stop, stop, stop," Porter protested.

They collapsed onto the asphalt, moaning. Finn noticed the stupid shopping cart that started this whole mess standing upright about three feet away from them. The rear of his SUV was sticking out of the front of the video store like it was mooning them. Then three City of Orange police cars, a fire engine, and an ambulance skidded to a stop in front of them. Men leaped out of the cars, barking orders. One cop spotted them and ran over.

"You guys okay?" He was an older white guy with a grey mustache. He kneeled down beside them.

"Yeah," they both said in unison.

"There's gas," Porter croaked.

"We've got it covered," the cop said. "You guys hurt?"

"I think I broke my leg." Porter said, his face twisted in pain.

The cop yelled for a medic and asked, "What happened? That SUV yours?"

Finn nodded.

The cop frowned. "Which one of you was driving?"

Without hesitation, Finn said, "Me."

Porter looked at him and the video store went *kaboom!*

SEVENTEEN

The reset was all a blur. They were both rushed to the ER, Porter for a broken femur and Finn for a concussion. Miraculously, they didn't have any other major injuries, although Finn's back was never the same again and he had to stop playing tennis.

Finn was charged with a DUI. His blood alcohol level was way over two times the legal limit at point-two. He was sentenced to community service and a hefty fine. Because he was a minor, he could have been sentenced to juvie, but it was his first offense so the judge granted him informal probation. He was ordered to attend alcohol awareness classes and his driver's license was suspended for one year which didn't matter because he didn't have a car anymore or anywhere to go.

The owner of the video store sued Finn's parents for obliterating his livelihood. It was a mom and pop store and worth nothing, but they got a hefty settlement from the insurance company.

Finn's dad yelled at him for what felt like a year. He'd never seen his dad so angry. Of course, no point in trying to get into Pepperdine now because what university would want a kid with shitty grades and a DUI on his record? Over time, the anger turned to resentment and finally indifference. Finn was a fucked-up loser in his dad's eyes and he knew his dad would never forgive him for embarrassing him. He tried to pretend he didn't give a shit that his dad barely acknowledged his existence, but it hurt like hell.

He and Porter talked about that night only once. It was the day Porter had his cast put on. His leg was hiked up in the air with a pulley thing. They were joking around, Porter laughing at Finn's imitation of the judge at his hearing. Porter got all quiet and looked serious.

"Why'd you do it?"

Finn shrugged. He felt stupid and didn't really want to talk about it. What was he supposed to say? Your life is worth so much more than my shitty one? You're going to be somebody and I'll never be anything?

"I don't know, man. Just instinct, I guess," he mumbled, refusing to meet Porter's intense gaze. "I know you'd do the same for me."

Porter didn't say anything, but Finn sensed him flinch underneath the thin hospital blanket. He would never forget those minutes that ticked by as the realization washed over him. He could still hear the steady hum of the hospital machines, the muted laughter out in the hallway. The smell of the harsh disinfectant.

Finn had never felt so alone in his entire life. Because it was then that he knew the truth. Porter would never have done what he did. Not in a million years. His best friend, the brother he never had but always wanted, wouldn't have stuck his neck out that far. Finn knew where he stood now and that killed him.

And even worse was that if it came down to it, Finn would do it all over again.

EIGHTEEN

Thinking about that day in the hospital always made Finn's insides clench. As if a parasite had wormed its way in and taken hold. The more he tried to ignore the hurt, the more it grew. The endless stream of hot chicks, booze, and drugs over the years did nothing to dissipate it. Only numbed him inside.

His friendship with Porter continued, of course, but it was never the same again, although it's not like Finn didn't hope or Porter didn't try. Sometimes for a moment, Finn felt as if everything was back to the way it was, like when they were kids. Like the time they were seven years old and rushed to the hospital for copycat concussions after leaping off Porter's roof in Superman capes. They had the best time eating ice cream together in their shared room. Or when both their dads missed their first varsity tennis match and they ended up ditching the game for Go Kart World.

Now it didn't matter. His best friend was dead and it was his fault. It had been over two weeks since Porter's murder, but each day it became more and more difficult for Finn to get out of bed and face a world without his best friend. A world he helped create.

But what Finn couldn't help wondering was would he have done things differently? Would he have turned himself in to the police in the very beginning to prevent Porter's murder?

At first, Finn told himself well, of course, he would have. Why *wouldn't* he save his best friend from a crazy psychopath? Wouldn't anyone else do the same? Wouldn't Porter?

Well, wouldn't he?

Finn realized it didn't matter what Porter would or wouldn't have done. Porter was gone and he wasn't ever coming back. From now on, all that mattered was what Finn would do.

NINETEEN

Mulling all this over at the end of a busy night at the restaurant, Finn made the decision to talk to Detective Wu first thing in the morning. He was getting tired of thinking about it and the only way to make it go away was to confront it, something he rarely did but shit, things change when your best friend's blood is on your hands. Even if that best friend wouldn't have done the same.

Just as Finn was about to leave for the night, he spotted a cell phone on his desk. The case was black with a white skull on the back. He picked it up to see if he could figure out whose it was but there was a password on it. Oh well. They'll come get it tomorrow, he figured.

He was preparing to lock up when he heard a noise in the kitchen. Was someone still here? Finn sighed and walked toward the back of the restaurant.

"I'm locking up," Finn announced. "Is that you,

Felipe?" His kitchen manager might still be around; he was such an anal freak when it came to prepping for the next morning. "Go home, dude."

Finn meandered around the kitchen but nobody was there. The black rubber mats were haphazardly thrown down on the kitchen tiles so he straightened them out. "Felipe?" Nothing.

Puzzled, he made his way toward the restrooms, wondering if a drunk customer had passed out or something, when he saw his office door slightly ajar. Even weirder was that the light was on inside, forming a bar of yellow on the red-tiled floor. He swore he had locked his door and turned the light off. The hair on the back of his neck stood up. He listened for any further noises but it was dead quiet except for the humming of the nearby ice machine.

Slowly, he inched his way toward his office. He let out a little yelp when the ice machine groaned. Feeling silly, he crept toward the open door, straining for any sounds that might indicate a guy waiting with a big ax to kill him. Maybe the noise he heard earlier was just the ice machine. But that didn't explain why his door was open.

When he was directly in front of his office, he pushed the door slightly. Crouched in front of the safe underneath his desk was a guy with a black beanie on his head. His Levis sagged so low, the top of his red plaid boxers were in plain sight. Looked like he was trying to open the safe. His head was bent down and Finn could hear the dial slowly turning. *Click, click, click.*

Finn was about to turn right back around, go outside, and call the police when he had a brilliant idea. Here was the perfect explanation for the missing five K. He would snap a quick photo and email it anonymously to corporate.

He pulled out his cell phone, made sure the volume was on mute so there wouldn't be the loud whirring of the camera, and snapped a photo of the guy on the floor.

What he didn't think of was his camera's powerful flash. Despite the light in his office, it was as if Finn had just launched a flash grenade into the tiny room. The burglar whirled around, leaping to his feet, with a "what the hell?" look on his face.

Then it was Finn's turn to look stunned. "Oscar?"

His former busser looked embarrassed, then covered it up with a scowl. He glanced down to the safe.

"You some kind of a safecracker now?" Finn felt relief and outrage at the same time. He checked the lock on his door but it didn't look tampered with. "And how'd you get in here anyway?"

The kid rolled his eyes. "Shit, everyone knows your code."

"They do?" He made a mental note to change it which was too bad. "ABC123" had been his code for years.

They stood there for a minute, eyeing each other warily until Finn sighed. "For Chrissakes, man, what the fuck?" He gripped Oscar's elbow and steered him toward the doorway. "Come on, asshole, I won't report you if you leave now. You're lucky I'm tired and just want to get the hell out of here." But if corporate decided to crack down on him for the stolen five K, he knew exactly what picture to show them.

Oscar yanked his arm back, glaring at Finn. "I ain't goin' nowhere with you, *esé*."

"Oh yeah?" Finn began then froze.

Oscar smirked.

Finn sniffed the air. Oscar reeked of pot like always, but he detected something else. Cheap cologne that made his stomach curdle. He'd never forget that smell.

"It was you." Anger bubbled inside Finn, but he struggled to sound indifferent. "You were in the car that night. You made the call."

The smug glint in Oscar's eyes confirmed it. He

couldn't help but gloat, the guy was a cocky son of a bitch.

"I fucking knew it." Finn wanted to grab the kid by the throat and bash his head against the wall. Then he remembered what Oscar said that night before he bolted out of the car.

"Why didn't you help Ronnie then if you saw us?"

"Maybe I did."

Oscar was his ticket to Ronnie. She might even be at his place right now. "Where is she, Oscar? Where's Ronnie?" He tried to keep his voice calm and steady.

The kid blew air out of the side of his mouth and shoved his hands deep into his jeans, sagging them even further. A small smile played at the corners of his mouth.

"Don't screw around with me, man." Finn got right into Oscar's weasel face. "I've got your file. I'll go to your place right now and if I find her there with my five K, you're in deep fucking shit." For the first time since this nightmare started, Finn was hopeful. He'd find Ronnie and haul her ass to the police.

Oscar chuckled. "Shit, man, she's long gone. And the five K."

"Where'd she go, Oscar?" He grabbed the front

of Oscar's shirt and shoved the scrawny kid against the wall. He was through being calm. "Where is she, you fuckin' wetback?" He shook Oscar until he heard his teeth rattle, his head bouncing off the wall. "Did you kill her?"

Oscar clutched at Finn's hands, trying to tear them off. "Naw, man. I didn't do shit."

Finn tossed Oscar aside like a used napkin and he crashed against Finn's desk. "Where's your girlfriend?" he yelled, towering over the kid. Finn had a good seven inches and seventy-five pounds on Oscar. He would beat the shit out of this idiot if he had to.

"She ain't my girlfriend," Oscar whined, lying on the desk. He coughed and struggled to right himself up. His T-shirt was all wrinkled in the front where Finn grabbed it. "I never met that crazy bitch until the day you fired me."

"Oh yeah? How?" Finn's fists clenched and unclenched at his sides, waiting. When Oscar didn't reply, Finn grabbed the front of his shirt, lifting him upright, and was about to pound his head against the wall again when Oscar pleaded, "Okay, okay. Take it easy."

Finn let go. Oscar crumpled against the desk. He hacked and wheezed, releasing a whiff of pot that made Finn's eyes water.

"She came up to me, man. I was smoking a cig outside the restaurant, fuckin' pissed, and she wanted a drag." Oscar straightened himself up, smoothing down his T-shirt. "We started talkin'. Told her about you firing me and your chicks in the hotel room." He chuckled. "Turns out she had a date with you the next night. It was fuckin' fate."

"Fate to do what? Rob me?"

"Naw, man. We were just gonna have a little fun. We thought it'd be funny to take your photo in your tighty-whities and then Instagram that shit. See what corporate thought of that. Maybe get your ass fired." He shook his head. "Then the bitch passed out." He shot Finn an accusatory look. "And you fuckin' left her there. That shit's cold."

Finn ignored that. "So then you decided to blackmail me."

Oscar shrugged. "Was too fuckin' easy, man."

"And here you are again, you pathetic piece of shit."

"That crazy bitch took it all," Oscar blurted. If Finn wasn't mistaken, he actually seemed hurt. "Took my fuckin' gun too, man," he muttered.

"So why don't you go after her and get it?"

"I can't go out there, man. I get seasick." Then Oscar looked like he'd said too much because his eyes widened, then narrowed.

Bingo. Finn mulled this new information over. It had to be an island. She could be on a boat but the way he said it. *I can't go out there.* Hawaii? No, Oscar could just fly there. It had to be an island that you could only access by boat.

Then he recalled Ronnie staring wistfully out at the land mass on the horizon that night.

"*I want to travel. Or even live on an island. Drink rum and eat coconuts every day.*"

Finn grinned. "Cata-fuckin'-lina."

Oscar hesitated, then shrugged. "What the fuck do I care? Yeah."

"You know where she's staying?" Excitement surged through Finn.

"Shit, man, I don't know."

But it didn't matter. All Finn wanted to do now was head to Catalina. He'd have to wait until morning, but right then, he wanted to get home and check the Catalina Express schedule for ferry departure times. "Okay, let's get the hell outta here. Forget this ever happened." He headed out of the office, grabbing Oscar's arm and dragging him with him. "C'mon, dipshit."

Oscar yanked his arm away and Finn turned to see him darting back inside the office.

"What the hell are you—?"

Oscar lunged down to the floor by the safe and

when he spun back around, he held up a pistol pointed right at Finn's gut.

Finn froze. "I thought you said Ronnie stole your gun."

"I got me a new one, smart ass."

Shit. Just his fucking luck.

TWENTY

"Get over here, *puta*, and open the fucking safe."

Finn hesitated, then walked into the office and crouched down in front of the safe, thinking. Maybe he could pretend he forgot the combination. Then what? He knew Oscar wouldn't buy that and would probably just shoot him in the back.

"Hurry up."

The gun dug into his spine. Finn touched the dial and spun. Slowly. Slowly. *Think, think.*

"Faster, *esé.*"

Finn spun the dial to the number three, then waited. The gun jabbed harder into his spine causing him to flinch.

"Don't fuck around, man."

"Mr. Roose?"

Finn turned to see Tomas' hulking frame standing in the doorway. Confusion clouded his bartender's angular features as he looked from Oscar to Finn, back to Oscar. He must have seen the gun then because his eyes widened. Without hesitation, Tomas tackled Oscar to the floor, grabbing for the gun. They both slammed into Finn.

Finn scuttled underneath the desk like a frightened mouse. He cowered there, watching Tomas and Oscar wrestling. Hard to tell what was going on or whose hands were gripping the gun. He grabbed his leather office chair that was rolling around in front of him to shield himself.

There was a loud *bang!* and something whizzed by Finn's right ear. He saw a small tuft of stuffing protruding from the back of the chair. Someone had shot through it. He turned to see a bullet lodged in the wall.

Another loud *bang!* and Finn turned to see Oscar lying still on the floor and Tomas holding the gun over him.

"I hated that guy," Tomas said.

Finn swallowed, wondering if he could just stay underneath the desk for the rest of his life. There was a strange whimpering sound and he realized it was coming from him.

Tomas peered underneath the desk at Finn.

"You come out now. It's okay. He's dead." His voice was devoid of emotion as usual.

Even when he's shooting people, he sounds like a robot. Unbelievable.

Finn scooted the chair forward and crawled out from underneath the desk warily. His ears were still ringing from the gunshots. Finn sucked in his breath when he saw Oscar lying in front of him. His eyes bulged out of his face, and his mouth was hanging open like he was in mid-scream. Dark liquid that Finn presumed was blood oozed out of a small hole in the middle of his forehead.

"Shit," Finn whispered. He felt like he was going to puke and realized he was trembling. It was the first time he'd seen a dead body. He never wanted to be this close to one ever again. He wrinkled his nose. "Fuck, what's that smell?"

Tomas was busy with his cell phone, seeming oblivious to the fact that he'd just shot someone. "Release of the bowels," he said in his monotone.

"Ew." Finn leaped up and scrambled out of the office into the hallway. His heart seemed to be beating out of his chest and he took a deep breath, struggling to calm down. He noticed Tomas had picked up the cell phone lying on his desk, the one with the skull case. "That your phone?" Finn asked.

Tomas had the phone up to his ear. He nodded. "I drive close by and see restaurant light still on."

Finn exhaled noisily. "Shit. Thank god you showed up, man. I can't even say how much I—"

Tomas began babbling in a foreign language into the phone. It sounded like Russian. Or Czech, although Finn had no idea what either of those languages sounded like. He heard unintelligible shouting through the phone. Apparently, the other person was a loud talker. After a few terse words, Tomas hung up the phone and turned his attention to Finn.

"You go."

Finn thought he heard him wrong. "Excuse me?" He looked down at Oscar. Blood was pooling underneath his head, slowly creeping toward the safe and the filing cabinet in the corner.

Tomas set the gun down on Finn's desk and began rifling through Oscar's pockets. He pulled out a wallet and a set of keys. He flipped the wallet open and pulled out a few crumpled dollar bills before tossing the empty wallet onto Finn's desk.

"What are you doing?" Finn felt like he was watching a movie. This wasn't really happening. "We have to call the police. Tell them what happened. It was an accident. Self-defense."

Tomas stuffed the cash into his jeans pocket. He tossed the keys onto the desk. "No police. You go. I take care of this."

Finn was flabbergasted. "Take care of this," he repeated. "What do you mean take care of this?"

"I am not going to jail again."

That pretty much confirmed the rumors about Tomas. Finn didn't even want to know what he'd done time for. Why HR didn't discover this in his background check was another mystery, but he wasn't going to take it up with them now.

"But Tomas. We have to report this. I mean—"

Tomas looked at Finn, his eyes cold and steel gray. "I just told you. I am not going to jail again."

Finn swallowed. "Okay."

"My brothers are on their way. You don't want to be here when they come."

Finn's eyes widened. *Seriously?*

"You don't worry. Okay?" Tomas nodded at Finn like he was a child.

Finn felt paralyzed. He knew he should call the police. It could all be explained as self-defense. But the last thing he wanted to do was piss off Tomas. And did he really want to meet his brothers? He nodded back. "Okay."

"Go," Tomas said.

Finn took one last look at Oscar's body, the pool of blood surrounding his head, the wet stain on the crotch of his former busser's jeans, and hauled ass out of there.

TWENTY-ONE

The next morning, Finn arrived at the Catalina Landing in Downtown Long Beach at 8 a.m. but the eight-thirty ferry ran only on weekends and it was a Monday so Finn had to wait until the ten o'clock ferry. He had called Courtney earlier, feigning a medical emergency and would she be a doll and cover for him? When he got to the part about shitting blood, she cut him off and quickly agreed to work a double, no problem.

It was chilly and overcast so very few people were milling around the Catalina Lounge waiting to board. Plus it was early October so tourist season was pretty much over.

Finn sat at a table with an espresso, in desperate need of a pick-me-up. He got very little sleep the night before, plagued with the image of Oscar and his tongue lolling out. He wondered what Tomas' brothers did with Oscar's body. He almost drove by the restaurant on the way to the ferry to check it out but then thought better of it. His mission right now was to go to Catalina and find Ronnie.

He wasn't sure how he was going to get her to the Redondo Beach Police. It's not like she would happily accompany him there. Maybe he'd have to incapacitate her somehow, tie her up. Then he'd call the police, let them figure out how to get her.

He wondered if he'd be able to see her again without losing it. Every time he pictured her impish smirk, he wanted to kill her. The bitch ruined his life. Took away his best friend. He kept reminding himself she was just a kid. A fucked-up kid, but a kid nonetheless.

When it was time to board the Catalina Express, Finn went up to the ferry's deck, gazing out at the muted grey horizon. Downtown Long Beach was directly behind him with the Pike, Long Beach's dining and retail center, and the aquarium looming in the distance.

He stood up on the deck the entire ride, not wanting to go down below to the rows of seats for fear of getting nauseous. It had happened before, although he blamed that on drinking one too many Buffalo Milks, Catalina's famous drink with vodka, coffee liqueur, and banana liqueur. He still couldn't look at a banana without gagging.

They docked in Avalon at the "mole" as locals

call it, which was essentially a pier where people fished. Finn walked down the gangway toward Crescent Street, the main drag. Avalon was the prime touristy area of Catalina Island and Finn prayed that's where Ronnie would be. If she chose the more reclusive Two Harbors, which was on the west side of the island where people camped and fished, then he'd be out of luck. He figured if he couldn't find her in Avalon, he'd stay the night and check out Two Harbors tomorrow.

Of course, that didn't cover the island's interior, which was filled with hiking trails, rougher terrain, and buffalo, the non-native animal famously brought over as "extras" for a film back in the 1920s. But Ronnie didn't seem the outdoorsy type or a big buffalo lover, so he didn't feel the need to check there right away.

As the day wore on, Finn began to realize how futile the search really was. Catalina was small but with nothing to go on, it was practically impossible for him to find her. She could be anywhere, hiding in a hotel room, a tent, a rundown bungalow. He might as well look for her in downtown Los Angeles or New York City.

He'd covered most of the popular restaurants and bars, figuring that's where someone like Ronnie would hang out. He poked his head in and showed her photo, the one the media and police used, to various restaurant servers and bartenders. All he got in return were head shakes, shrugs, and blank stares. Lively bunch, the islanders. He checked hotels, gift shops, and places where you could rent snorkeling gear. Each time he showed Ronnie's photo, he received the same response: a whole lot of nothing.

Exhausted by the end of the day, he collapsed on a chaise lounge at the Descanso Beach Club, a beach east of the famous dome-shaped Avalon Casino. It had to be close to five-thirty, the sun barely visible with all the clouds and fog. A breeze chilled him and he wished he'd brought a warmer jacket. He just hadn't planned to be there all day.

Actually, he hadn't planned at all. What did he expect? Ronnie to come running toward him, yelling, "Here I am!"? Yeah, that would have been nice.

"Can I get you a drink?"

Finn looked up to see a young woman with a short black bob hovering over him. She had dark sunglasses on despite the dreary day and was wearing an orange polo with the Descanso Beach Club logo. Her smile wavered, then disappeared.

"Yes, please." The more Finn thought about it, the more he wanted a drink. No, he *needed* a drink.

"What beers do you have?"

She rattled off the list of beers and nothing sounded good to Finn.

"I'll have a Jack and coke." Then he added, "Make that a double."

She nodded and spun around, hurrying away.

He sank back into the club's beach chair, overwhelmed with fatigue and despair. It was quiet except for the faint sound of leaves rustling and someone laughing in the distance. The damp air seemed to seep right into his thin windbreaker and he shivered.

"Here you go, sir."

A tall tan guy in the Descanso Beach Club orange polo appeared beside Finn. He handed Finn his drink and then offered a menu. "Would you like to order some food as well?"

Finn took the drink and swallowed a big gulp. Ah, that was more like it. He grabbed the menu, wincing at how sticky it was. "Where's Little Miss Sunshine?"

The tan guy laughed. "Oh, you mean Cherry? She told me to take over. Probably too hung-over from Buccaneer Days."

At the mention of Cherry, Finn froze. *Cherry Nibbles.* Then again, that would be too fucking easy.

"She still around? Can you find her for me?"

The server hesitated, probably thinking Finn was some kind of pervert. He mumbled something about giving Finn a minute and scurried off.

Finn stood up, scouring the beach for Cherry. The sun had just gone down, leaving an overcast pall across the harbor. Moored boats of various sizes bobbed up and down in the water, a few with lights on illuminating people milling around on-board. Otherwise, the beach was deserted.

Just when he was about to leave the shore to search around the bar, he spotted her. She was scooting a kayak into the water about a hundred or so feet away from him, wearing the same stupid orange shirt. She was about knee-deep in the water, her hand guiding the kayak out toward the ocean. As if she could sense Finn watching, she turned and stared right at him. She no longer wore the dark sunglasses.

Finn sucked in his breath. *You gotta be shittin' me.* It was definitely Ronnie. He sprinted after her.

TWENTY-TWO

What he didn't count on was how rocky the shore was. He ended up slipping and sliding around on his flip-flops like a drunk dancer. He waved his arms and yelled.

"Hey! Ronnie!"

Ronnie turned back to look at him before stepping into the kayak and pushing off into the ocean with her oar.

"Wait!" Finn watched helplessly as her kayak careened off into the water, already too far away for him to run or swim to. It was a little choppy and she was struggling to control the swaying kayak with her oar. She turned around again. Then the bitch grinned and waved at him.

"Shit." He looked around—several kayaks lined up along the shore like runners waiting to take off at the starting line. He ran over to one and scooted it out into the water. He couldn't remember the last time he kayaked, but it couldn't be that hard.

He stepped into the kayak, or at least he thought he did, but the fucking thing kept moving around on him. "For god's sake," he muttered. Why couldn't there have been a row of jet skis waiting here?

It was getting darker by the second and Ronnie was a bobbing figure in the distance, about a couple hundred feet ahead of him. Pretty soon, she'd be impossible to spot.

"Shit!" Frustrated, Finn just ran into the ocean, pushing the kayak along with him until the water was up to his waist. He flung himself onto the kayak and hung on for dear life. The waves seemed to move the kayak in one direction and his body in another, but he managed to maneuver his way into a sitting position.

He grasped the oar and paddled like a madman after Ronnie.

He could still see her way up ahead. She kept turning around to check on him and the movement of her head was like a beacon that Finn followed.

"Ronnie! Where the hell are you going? You can't kayak forever!" Shit, he knew *he* couldn't. But he sure as hell would try.

For a second, he didn't see her and panicked. He pushed his oar into the water, going out to sea as fast as he could. He knew she was out there somewhere. His shoulders were sore and his back ached more than usual, but he just kept going. Now that the sun was down, the temperature seemed to drop about twenty degrees or maybe it was because Finn was soaked, his clothes clinging to him like papier-mâché.

He paddled past anchored yachts and sailboats and was tempted to yell and ask for help but then what would he say? "Help me catch that girl, she's getting away!" wasn't exactly something people would respond to. Plus, most of the boats looked dark and empty.

He scanned the harbor and almost missed her but spotted movement near a sailboat moored in the water about a hundred feet ahead. He paddled ferociously toward the boat, sweating despite the chill, and when he got close enough he saw her kayak adrift in the water with nobody in it. Apparently, she'd either boarded the boat or decided to take a plunge into the ocean.

Then he spotted her on the bow of the sailboat, looking down at him.

"Ronnie! This is stupid." He craned his neck up at her. "Will you just stop this?"

"Stop what?"

"Running away like this. Why don't you want to go home?"

"I don't need to explain myself to you."

Finn sighed. This wasn't going the way he'd hoped. Plus every time he looked up at her, he'd get dizzy from the bobbing kayak. He tried another approach. "Think about your mom. She's worried about you."

Ronnie snorted. "So."

She obviously didn't give a shit about her mom. Finn thought of something else. "In a few months, you'll be eighteen, and then you can go wherever you want. I doubt your mom would be able to make you do something you don't want to do."

She was silent, then she said, "It's not my mom I'm worried about."

"Your dad? He's in jail."

She shook her head. "It's not my dad either." She paused. "It's my uncle."

"Your uncle?" Finn didn't realize there was another relative in the picture. "Does he...?" He almost said "abuse you" but then he felt awkward. Instead, he said, "Would he come after you?"

"Yes," she replied. "And he would never give up."

That sounded ominous. Before he could ask her more questions, she leaned down and he heard the loud rumbling of an engine cut through the harbor like a siren. She was preparing to leave. Finn panicked.

"Look, let's just talk some more, okay?"

She shrugged. "Fine by me. Come aboard."

Finn wasn't expecting that. He scanned the harbor, the boats scattered like an obstacle course. The nearest boat was pretty close to them, about fifty feet away, with its lights on, blasting Bon Jovi's "Livin' on a Prayer." He shivered. Now that he'd stopped paddling, his body was cooling off and his wet clothes weren't helping.

"I can give you something dry to change into," Ronnie offered. "Then we can chat some more."

"How do I know you don't have a gun?" He thought of Oscar's gun, the one he claimed she stole from him.

She sighed, exasperated. "Why would I shoot you, huh? You think I'm afraid of you?"

"You must be. You ran away like a fugitive." He paused, then added, "And not the stealthiest getaway, I must say."

She cocked her head at him. "Who said I was going for stealthy?"

Finn thought about that. Was she purposely luring him out here? In the middle of the ocean so she could kill him? It actually made sense. He was the only one who knew she was out here, aside from Oscar who wouldn't be coming out to Catalina anytime soon.

"I'll take you back to the mainland if you hurry the hell up," she added. "Otherwise, I'm leaving your dumb ass here."

"Fine, how do I get up there?"

"Paddle over here. There's a ladder." She pointed to the other side of the boat, behind her.

Finn obeyed, paddling around the bow of her boat until he spotted the metal ladder. He noticed the boat's name was Vagabond. He guided the kayak over and carefully stood, grabbing the ladder's sides and climbing up. Ronnie hovered above him and grabbed his arm, pulling him onto the deck.

"Jesus, you're soaked. What'd you do, kayak underneath the water?"

"I didn't exactly have time to step into the kayak gracefully, okay?"

"Wait here." Ronnie disappeared down the stairs into the cabin.

Finn looked around the boat. It was small, maybe a twenty-seven-foot sailboat, and desperately needed refinishing. The diesel engine whined loudly.

Ronnie popped up from the galley below, now wearing a bulky gray hoodie over her Descanso polo. She handed him sweats as she climbed all the way onto the deck. "I think those'll fit. You're pretty small from what I remember."

Finn chose to ignore that jab and peeled off his wet windbreaker and his T-shirt. Shivering, he yanked the sweatshirt on. He peeled his khakis and boxers off, not caring that Ronnie was watching him—it's not like she hadn't seen him already—and pulled the sweatpants on. They were a little snug and short but they were warm and most importantly, dry. He glanced down at his ensemble. They were faded but most definitely pink.

"Wonderful," he grumbled.

"Hey, at least they're dry," Ronnie said with a grin. "You look kinda cute."

Finn glowered at her.

Ronnie's grin faded. "I figured you'd find me eventually. I was kind of waiting."

"Oh yeah?" He didn't know how to reply to that. "Waiting for what?"

After a pause, she replied, "I don't like what-ifs."

"What 'what-ifs'?"

"So how'd you find me anyway?" she asked, ignoring his question. "That dickwad rat me out?"

"If you mean Oscar, then yes."

"I knew it. Couldn't keep his big mouth shut."

She glanced around. "He here?"

Finn shook his head. "He's dead."

Ronnie didn't look surprised. In fact, she didn't react at all. "Sucks to be him."

"I thought you two were friends." He didn't mention the part about Oscar calling her a "crazy bitch."

Ronnie snorted. "Yeah, right. He just used me to get what he wanted."

"The way you used me." It wasn't a question.

A small smile tugged on the corners of Ronnie's mouth. "That was different. I actually had fun with you." She shrugged.

Finn was taken aback and slightly suspicious. At this point, he figured everything about that night on the boat—sharing their failures, their dreams, the passion—was all a big setup. What was real and what was fake?

She seemed to read his mind again. "Everything I said to you that night was true. Everything I felt." She said the last part so quietly that Finn had to strain to hear her over the idling engine. Plus the loud music from the other boat, which was now Guns N Roses' "Welcome to the Jungle."

Finn snorted. "Bullshit."

"I'm telling you the truth. Honest." She shook her head. "I never wanted to screw you over. I actually liked you. Thought you were cute." She smiled. "I still do." Slowly, she approached him.

Finn instinctively backed up, then felt stupid. He wasn't afraid of this chick. Okay, maybe a little.

"Wouldn't you wanna try one last time, huh?" Ronnie licked her lips, coming closer. Closer. "I think we both know how amazing it would be. Come down below with me."

She was only a few feet away from him. He could tackle her, maybe hit her over the head and tie her up. He glanced around for something to knock her out with.

"I know you want me, Finnie," she said. She stepped closer and one hand reached out, grabbing his cock. Shit.

He heard a moan and realized it was coming from him. She stood right in front of him, they were practically touching noses. She pressed her tits against his chest and snaked her hand inside the sweatpants, stroking his cock.

"Let's go down to the cabin," she whispered, her eyes half-closed, beckoning him. "Let's get naked and fuck our brains out."

"Welcome to the Jungle" from the nearby party boat reverberated in Finn's head, his entire body. He knew he shouldn't go downstairs. It was a trap. But god, whatever she was doing with her hand felt so fucking good. He felt himself relax.

Ronnie pulled him toward her. "Come down below with me, okay?" She sounded annoyed now.

Warning bells went off in his head as he stumbled forward. The sexual allure was gone from her eyes now, replaced by hardened resolve. Finn shoved her away and she flew backwards but quickly recovered, bringing something out from her hoodie front pocket. A gun pointed directly at his gut.

TWENTY-THREE

Finn groaned. He fucking knew it. "I thought you weren't going to shoot me."

"And you believed me?" She scoffed at him. "Come on, Finn. You should know better than that."

"So all this about liking me, having fun, was a crock of shit?" He immediately regretted asking. He sounded pathetic.

"I did have fun." She shrugged. "But so what? Like I said, I don't like what-ifs." She glanced to her right and Finn knew she was gauging how loud the gunshot would be. Would it be drowned out by the party boat's loud music? She must have decided the other boat was too close. She edged toward the stern, her arm steady, pointing the gun at him.

"Sit down."

Finn shuffled over to his right and sat down. The boat's seat cushions were worn thin and it felt like he was sitting directly on the fiberglass. Ronnie leaned down to the engine controls and pushed the throttle forward, her eyes and the gun still trained on him. The engine whined loudly but the boat didn't budge.

"We're going on a little trip," she said.

Finn remained where he was, watching her struggle with the throttle. She obviously had no clue what she was doing. Sure, she had the throttle pushed forward, which was like a car's accelerator, but she had the gear shift in neutral so the boat wouldn't go anywhere no matter how hard she gunned the engine.

"Goddammit," she muttered. "Fucking stupid thing." She kept swiveling her head back and forth, looking at him and then down at the throttle and gear shift.

"You have to push the gear away from you," Finn instructed.

"Shut up!" Ronnie turned to him, the gun leveled now at his head.

Finn threw his hands up. "I'm just trying to help."

She scowled, then glanced down at the controls. "Which one's the gear shift?" she finally asked.

"The one with the black knob." Finn paused. "Your throttle has the red knob." The engine rumbled so roughly that Finn could feel it in his entire body as if he were sitting on a speaker at an outdoor rock concert.

"Hm." Ronnie put her hand on the gear shift and then narrowed her eyes at him. "You wouldn't be lying to me now, would you?" Her gun arm stiffened.

"Jesus, I'm telling you that's the gear shift. Push it forward." He pointed.

Ronnie frowned, glanced down at the controls, then back at Finn. She seemed hesitant.

"That's right. Just push it forward." He casually gripped the guardrail behind him.

She gave him one last glare before shoving the gear shift forward. Instantly, the boat jerked and then flew forward with such force that it catapulted Finn off his seat. Thank god he'd been gripping the guardrail otherwise he would have flown overboard. He figured the boat would either take off like a rocket or stall but he wasn't expecting this.

Ronnie, meanwhile, had been flung to the deck and was struggling to stand up but the speed of the boat was making it practically impossible. She gripped the boom, hoisting herself up and swaying like a drunk.

"What the fuck?" she screamed. "You tricked me! You fuckin' tricked me!"

"Turn the engine off!" Finn screamed, pointing

at the ignition key. Ronnie was right next to it.

"What?"

"The engine! Turn it off!" Finn pointed but Ronnie was staring at something ahead of them, a grim look on her face. Finn turned to find that they were hurtling directly at another little sailboat and they didn't have much time until they T-boned it.

Finn lunged for the throttle, pulling it back to idle. It slowed down but he wasn't fast enough. They crashed into the other boat with a sickening *crunch.* The impact flung him forward and water sprayed him in the face as he crumpled to the deck. He struck his head on something hard.

"Oof." He reached for the back of his head and winced in pain. That's when he saw the gun about five feet away from him. He locked eyes with Ronnie who was lying on the seat cushions, soaking wet.

As if someone yelled "go," they both dove for the gun. Finn almost had it but Ronnie stomped on his hand with her tennis shoe.

He clutched his fingers, howling in pain.

Ronnie reached down to pick up the gun and Finn, ignoring the burning pain in his hand, latched onto her leg, pulling her toward him. She kicked viciously at him, but he held on and she slipped on the wet deck, falling against the cabin with a *thud.*

Finn tackled her, going for the gun in her hand. They wrestled like that for a while, both of their hands on the gun, then there was a loud *bang*. Something whistled past his face, momentarily stunning him. He shook his head trying to get rid of the buzzing sound. There was another *bang* but it sounded further away, he couldn't really tell, then Ronnie was on top of him and god, she was still fucking heavy. Finn elbowed her in the face and he heard a crack, her head flying back.

She screamed. Her hands flew to her face, releasing the grip on the gun.

He hoped he broke her nose. He thrust his knee up and shoved her off of him. She flew back pretty easily. Finn leaped up onto his feet holding the gun, then stumbled. He glanced down and saw a dark stain on the left thigh of the pink sweatpants.

"You fucking shot me!" Finn staggered toward Ronnie, the gun pointed at her. "You bitch."

"You fucking broke my nose." Ronnie lay on the deck, whimpering like a wounded animal. Blood covered her face so he could barely make out her features. "And you ruined my boat."

There was water everywhere. It gushed into the boat and they listed to one side. If they stayed onboard for even five more minutes, they'd sink into the ocean. The boat they crashed into was almost split in half and already partially submerged in the water.

"Shit." Finn looked around wildly, trying to figure out how far they were from shore. Okay, pretty fucking far. He noticed Ronnie trying to climb up onto the edge of the boat, blood oozing from her nose. The crazy bitch was going to jump.

"Where the hell are you going? I've got a gun. I'll fucking shoot you."

"So fucking shoot me then."

Finn aimed at Ronnie. He'd never shot anyone before. But no way was he letting her get away.

"I'm warning you," he yelled. He stretched his arm out further, aiming for her back, the gun shaking in his hand. "Goddammit!" He tossed the gun aside, frustrated. He couldn't shoot her. Not in the back. Jesus.

Ignoring the pain in his thigh, he lunged for Ronnie's legs just as she stood upright on the edge. She kicked at him, trying to get him off of her, and the rubber sole on the bottom of her shoe nailed him in the forehead.

"Goddammit!" Finn gripped her legs even harder and pulled her toward him.

"Let go of me!" she cried, squirming and kicking, gripping onto the guardrail.

"Stay put. Help is on its way," a voice on a

megaphone called out. It sounded close.

Startled, Finn looked around and spotted a speedboat to his right, hurtling toward them. The word "Sheriff" in bold black letters was on the side. Thank god. They were only about fifty feet away.

Ronnie took advantage of Finn's distraction and kicked him in the face again, this time directly in the eye.

Finn yelped and reached for his face, letting go of Ronnie's legs. He heard a splash and peered over the edge of the boat with his one good eye. She was somewhere in that frigid cold water, but it was so dark, he couldn't see shit.

"Ronnie!" He didn't hear splashing. He limped over to the boat's port side and gazed out into the water but there was only bottomless blackness. He gave up and sank onto the seat cushion. The pain in his leg had worsened and he could barely move it without crying.

He heard shouting and the sound of the speedboat engine coming closer, closer. Finn closed his eyes and lay down on the seat, feeling himself drifting off. After what seemed like a year but was probably only two minutes, the sound of heavy footsteps and shouting startled him. He opened his eyes to see three men staring down at him.

"We want to see your hands, sir."

Finn realized they were all deputies and one of them had a gun pointed at him. He raised his hands up, wiggling his fingers weakly.

"Is this your boat, sir?"

"Is this your gun?"

"Are you shot?"

"Is there anyone else on board?"

Everyone was peppering him with questions and all he could do was close his eyes and moan.

"Medic!" one deputy yelled.

Suddenly a paramedic was beside him, asking Finn questions, like if he knew his name.

"Ronnie is—"

"Ronnie? That your name, sir?"

"No, no, no, she's in the water." He tried to sit up and point but it was too painful so he lay back down.

"Who?" This was the first deputy again.

"Sir, what's your name?" repeated the medic.

"Ronnie—" he began again.

"Ronnie, what's your last name?"

"Oh god," Finn groaned and gave up.

"Someone's in the water. Over there!" a deputy shouted.

"Finally," Finn mumbled.

More shouting and then he heard a splash.

Someone must have dove overboard to get her.

Strong hands grabbed him and carried him off the boat. His leg felt like it was on fire. He saw two deputies hovering over the edge of the boat and shouting. Eventually, Finn was laid down gently on something hard and saw that he was lying in a giant speedboat.

"We're almost there, sir. Hang in there." A young paramedic was busying himself around Finn, adjusting him and Finn felt something soft underneath his head.

He nodded. He heard the revving of a powerful engine and then they were flying. People kept asking him what his name was and where he was hurt. Finn pointed to his leg and when he saw the pink sweatpants soaked in blood, he almost passed out.

They docked at the pier and two paramedics lifted him out, lowering him onto a waiting gurney. Someone gave him a shot of something and he flinched. Hopefully it was some fucking morphine.

He laid back on the gurney, staring up into the night sky. He couldn't see any stars. People shouted instructions and it was general chaos around him but he felt like he was floating up, up, up and away from it all. The pain in his leg slowly subsided.

A round face loomed above him. Holy shit, Finn

knew that face. Jackson, the fucking P.I., his expression inscrutable as usual.

"What the hell are you doing here?" Finn mumbled. It came out more like "whashelloo-dongear?" He tried sitting up to get a better look but it felt like he was underwater.

"I've been following you. I knew you'd lead me right to Ronnie."

Finn groaned. Felt like he was falling backwards. The last thing he remembered before he blacked out was Jackson's eyes, like two little round coals, peering down at him.

TWENTY-FOUR

Finn stayed in the Catalina Island Medical Center overnight and surprisingly all he needed was thirteen stitches in his thigh and five in the back of his head. The bullet merely grazed his leg, nothing more.

Jackson even paid him a visit.

"So how long you been following me?" Finn asked. He'd found Jackson sitting solemnly by his bedside when he came out of the bathroom, legs crossed like a woman.

Jackson shrugged, his jacket shifting slightly. "Since the day we chatted at the restaurant."

The little man had to be bullshitting him. "I would have noticed you."

"Everyone thinks that."

That pissed Finn off even more. "Why?"

"Why what?"

Finn blew out a noisy sigh. "Why did you follow me?"

"Because I knew you were lying."

"How did you know that?"

"It's what I do."

"Did you know Ronnie was still alive?"

"Did you?"

"I had a feeling," Finn replied.

"So did I."

The P.I. stood up and tugged his jacket down over his belly. "Well, you seem fine." Jackson turned to go.

"Wait a second. Where's Ronnie? Is she alive?"

"She's alive."

"Is she going to jail?"

Jackson shrugged. "It's an ongoing investigation and she refuses to tell us anything." He paused. "But they'll most likely arraign her. Then send her to Los Padrinos."

"Where?"

"The juvie center in Whittier."

Finn was disappointed. He was hoping for hard core prison time.

"I'm sure someone from the sheriff's will be in soon to talk to you," the P.I. added before leaving his room.

Ten minutes later, Deputy Stone, the same one who had asked him what his name was on the boat last night, came into Finn's room and sat down. He wanted to know how Finn knew Rhonda Havemeyer so Finn told him.

He started with that fateful day Ronnie walked into his restaurant. How they went sailing the next night on the Moonshine, while carefully omitting all the lewd details. Technically nothing happened anyway. When he got to the part about leaving her at the marina because she was so young and he was drunk, Finn expected the deputy to comment. Instead, he just silently listened. Even when he talked about Porter and how guilty he felt for indirectly getting his best friend killed, the deputy remained stoic.

Finn concluded with how he tracked Ronnie down to Catalina and she tried to kill him, being sure to leave out any mention of Oscar and the blackmail scheme. When he finished with the gunshot and the boat crash from last night, Deputy Stone slowly closed his notebook. Finn noticed the deputy hadn't jotted a single thing down.

"That's quite a story, Mr. Roose."

"It's all true."

The deputy nodded. "Sounds like I'm the first one you told." He cleared his throat. "The statements from Mr. Jackson and the witnesses from the party boat corroborate what you've just told me.

My advice to you is to leave our island immediately and go home."

"That's it?"

The deputy stood up. "The people whose boat you obliterated may try to sue you but that's not my concern." He headed for the doorway.

"What about Redondo Beach PD?"

Deputy Stone turned around. "We've contacted them. Manhattan Beach PD too."

"And?"

The deputy shrugged. "Who knows? They'll probably want to talk to you about withholding information or impeding an investigation, but cowardly scumbags like you may not be worth their time."

"I hope you're right."

The deputy shook his head and left the room.

Finn was released that afternoon, clothed in Ronnie's blood-stained pink sweats, and after filling out the proper paperwork, a nurse arrived with a wheelchair, ready to take him outside.

"I don't need that."

"It's hospital policy," she said with a bright smile.

"Oh fine," Finn grumbled. "Whatever."

As she wheeled him down the hospital corridor, Finn heard a girl talking loudly from the private room up ahead. He recognized that voice.

"Wait a second." The nurse stopped and Finn leaped out of the wheelchair, darting inside the room. Ronnie sat up in the hospital bed, a white bandage on her nose. Jackson perched at her bedside.

"Tell my mom not to come," Ronnie was saying. They both turned to look at Finn. Ronnie glared.

"What are you doing here?" she snapped.

"Just wanted to say enjoy juvie. I hear it's great."

"Fuck you."

"I don't think this is a good idea, Mr. Roose." Jackson stood up, looking ready to toss Finn outside. "My niece here is having a hard enough time as it is without you antagonizing her."

"Mr. Roose, you need to leave," ordered the nurse behind him.

Finn ignored her, trying to comprehend what the private detective just said. "Your niece?" He looked at Ronnie, then pointed at Jackson. "*This* guy is your uncle?"

Ronnie rolled her eyes. "Good job, Sherlock."

Finn felt his mouth hanging open and quickly closed it. Jackson was her uncle? It made sense though once he thought about it. Obviously, the little man was good at finding people, like Ronnie said. And it explained how Ronnie's parents could afford a P.I. Still, he just couldn't see any sign of an abusive uncle. Sure, Jackson was a little intense and annoying, but he certainly didn't seem like the type to harm anyone.

"I don't get it," Finn said. "What am I missing here?"

"What do you mean?" Jackson asked.

"Ronnie here made it sound like you were creepy Uncle Fester. You seem normal to me."

"Thank you."

Ronnie scoffed.

"Mr. Roose." The nurse sounded pissed now.

"So what's the deal, huh?" Finn ignored her. "Why run away?"

"My niece here doesn't seem to appreciate my insistence she attend college. And make something of herself." Jackson shook his head. "She insists on being—" using air quotes, "—free."

"You're such an ass!" Ronnie yelled, her pretty face turned grotesque with rage. "Why can't you just leave me alone?"

"Mr. Roose, it's time for you to go." The nurse grabbed Finn's arm and led him back outside to the hallway, plunking him down into the wheelchair with a huff.

"Ouch." His stitches were still sore but clearly

the nurse had run out of patience and sympathy.

When Finn emerged from the medical center into the gray afternoon, he spotted a sheriff car idling in the street. He recognized Deputy Stone in the driver's seat.

"Mr. Roose?" The deputy waved his hand out the window. "Get in. I'll take you to the pier."

"You don't trust me to go by myself, I take it."

The deputy shot Finn a look that he recognized. Disgust. "Let's just say I want to personally escort you off our island. We'll be in touch with you on Ronnie's court case; otherwise, I'd be okay with never seeing you again."

When they arrived at the pier, Deputy Stone pointed to the Catalina Express.

"That's your boat. I suggest you get on it."

After thanking the deputy, Finn trudged up the pier toward the ferry. He purchased a ticket and boarded, one of the last people on, and made his way up onto the deck. The ferry pulled out into the water, cruising slowly, and Finn sucked in a lungful of sea air. People gave him funny looks, probably the bloody pink sweats, but he didn't care.

He called Courtney to apologize for lying yesterday. He swore he'd make it up to her, his polite tone and honesty clearly something she wasn't used to. She sighed and told him in her clipped tone to just come into work already and they'd deal with it then. He reassured her he was now heading home, but he'd be at the restaurant in a couple of hours. *Unless Detective Wu is waiting for me with handcuffs.*

He was prepared for it though. He was through with picking up women, through with being a selfish prick. No more hotel rooms, fast cars, and yachts. What good came of it besides thirteen stitches in his thigh and five more in his head? And of course, the unrelenting guilt.

He even called Sharla, the redheaded massage therapist, and told her things wouldn't work out between them.

"I'm probably going to jail anyway so we shouldn't start anything," he said. He hung up before she could reply. Best to start his life as the new and improved Finn with a clean slate. It actually felt good to tell the truth.

Finn's stomach did flip flops when the ferry docked an hour later and he scanned the parking lot for Detective Wu but the Asian cop wasn't there. Nobody from the Redondo Beach PD nor Manhattan Beach PD was there. He should have felt relief but somehow it made him more nervous. Maybe they were waiting for him at the restaurant. Well, he was ready for them.

When he pulled up to his apartment building, he noticed an attractive woman in a conservative business suit stepping out of a Lexus, carrying some papers. Finn parked on the street and got out of his Saab, heading to the front of his building.

"Mr. Roose?"

Finn turned around and the woman's face registered amusement as she looked him up and down.

"Yes?" Finn wondered if she was a new detective on the case. Maybe she was Manhattan Beach PD.

"Phineas Roose?" She didn't seem convinced.

"Yes, can I help you?" He figured she was thrown off by his outfit, but if she was with the police, wouldn't she already know what happened?

The woman smiled and cleared her throat. "I apologize for ambushing you like this but when I went to your restaurant, the manager there said you were on your way home."

"Yes, and here I am." He just wanted her to handcuff him and get it over with.

"I'm from the Law Officcs of Neiswender and Smith." She paused. "We're handling the estate of Porter Steadman and he's named you as the successor to his 2012 Ferrari California and forty-four-foot yacht, the Moonshine."

Finn shook his head, unsure he heard her correctly.

"We're trying to wrap this up quickly for Mrs. Steadman and had difficulty finding you so I apologize again for the sudden notice but—well, here you go." She pulled something from her jacket pocket and dangled a set of keys.

Finn stuck out his hand, and she dropped them into his open palm.

"Will you just sign here?" She thrust the papers at him.

Finn stared at the papers, then at the keys in his hand. He felt a grin stretch across his face. Shoving the keys in his pocket, he signed the papers with a flourish and said, "So what are you doing later tonight, darling?"

ACKNOWLEDGMENTS

I want to give a huge thank you to my tireless writer group, Travis Richardson and Stephen Buehler. You guys are responsible for making Finn something I can be proud of.

Thanks goes to Matt Coyle for reading an early draft and giving me indispensable notes.

Thank you to Sergeant Tim Colson for patiently answering my endless questions on police investigations and the court system. Any inaccuracies are entirely on me.

I'm eternally grateful for Brian Benbenek's amazing resourcefulness and unwavering support despite the whole ex-husband thing.

A big thank you to Chris Rhatigan and Mike Monson of All Due Respect Books for believing in Finn and loving him as much as I do.

Finally, I am indebted to Darrell James, the very first person to read Finn and encourage me to keep going. I can't thank you enough.

Sarah M. Chen juggles several jobs including indie bookseller, transcriber, and insurance adjuster. Her crime fiction short stories have been accepted for publication online and in various anthologies, including *All Due Respect*, *Akashic*, *Plan B*, *Shotgun Honey*, *Crime Factory*, *Out of the Gutter*, *Betty Fedora*, *Spelk*, and *Dead Guns Press*. *Cleaning Up Finn* is her first book.

https://sarahmchen.com/

OTHER TITLES FROM ALL DUE RESPECT

See AllDueRespectBooks.com for complete list

By Greg Barth
Selena: Book One
Diesel Therapy: Book Two
Suicide Lounge: Book Three
Road Carnage: Book Four
Everglade: Book Five

By Eric Beetner
Nine Toes in the Grave

By Phil Beloin Jr.
Revenge is a Redhead

By Math Bird
Histories of the
Dead and Other Stories

By Paul D Brazill
The Last Laugh: Crime Stories

By Sarah M. Chen
Cleaning Up Finn

By Alec Cizak
Crooked Roads: Crime Stories
Manifesto Destination

By Pablo D'Stair
and Chris Rhatigan
You Don't Exist

By C.S. DeWildt
Kill 'Em with Kindness
Love You to a Pulp

By Paul Heatley
FatBoy

By Jake Hinkson
The Deepening Shade

By Preston Lang
The Sin Tax

By Marietta Miles
Route 12

OTHER TITLES FROM ALL DUE RESPECT

See AllDueRespectBooks.com for complete list

By Mike Miner
Prodigal Sons

By Mike Monson
A Killer's Love
Criminal Love and Other Stories
Tussinland
What Happens in Reno

By Matt Phillips
Three Kinds of Fool
Accidental Outlaws

By Rob Pierce
The Things I Love Will Kill Me Yet: Stories
Uncle Dust
Vern in the Heat
With the Right Enemies

By Michael Pool
Debt Crusher

By Chris Rhatigan
Race to the Bottom
Squeeze
The Kind of Friends Who Murder Each Other

By Ryan Sayles
I'm Not Happy 'til You're Not Happy: Crime Stories

By Ryan Sayles and Chris Rhatigan
Two Bullets Solve Everything

By Daniel Vlasaty
A New and Different Kind of Pain
Only Bones

By William E. Wallace
Dead Heat with the Reaper
Hangman's Dozen

Made in the USA
Lexington, KY
03 October 2018